Gecko Keck

BAYALA

The Daughters of the Elf King

schleich Ⓢ

Impressum

BAYALA
The Daughters of the Elf King

Author and graphic designer:
Gecko Keck

Translated from German into English:
STAR Deutschland GmbH

Unabridged edition published by
Schleich GmbH 2008
All rights reserved.

Address:
Schleich GmbH
Am Limes 69
73527 Schwäbisch Gmünd
Germany

schleich@schleich-s.de

www.schleich-s.de

ISBN 978-3-9812518-5-2

The Land of the Elves

lves, fairies, witches, trolls and dwarves – all these magical creatures have one thing in common: they are mysterious beings whose origins often go back hundreds of years.

The real world of the elves is alien to human beings. It lies far beyond any reality in a place which no human has ever seen.

Elves themselves call this place, or rather this country, "Bayala" which means "the land of a thousand faces" in their language. The name stems from the fact that the land changes enchantingly from north to south and new and wonderful landscapes are opened up continuously.

The far north is dominated by huge mountain ranges with almost inaccessible snowy peaks. Wide rivers flow and entrancing, crystal clear mountain streams meander in the deep valleys and gorges surrounding this enormous mountain massif.

The elves in the north, the so-called "Shadow Elves", have adapted to these surroundings. They have strong feathered wings for better movement in the harsh natural environment. The deep valleys in this region receive much less sunlight than the more southern regions of the land. The skin of the Shadow Elves is therefore much lighter and more sensitive, while their hair is often black or dark brown. Their horses also have the same characteristics. Large noble stallions or mares with a dark fine coat are the constant companions of Shadow Elves. Shadow Elves are by nature rather melancholic and introverted. This also means that they wear dark clothes made of heavy black, brown or red materials. Golden or bronze coloured ornaments decorate their boots, coats or skirt hems and conceal symbols that have a magical meaning.

Shadow Elves live in steep rock caves, which rise up into the sky like pinnacles and whose form is almost indistinguishable from the surrounding mountains. Inside the rock caves are small volcanic craters which give off warmth and bathe the barren rooms in a warm red light.

The further south you go, the flatter and more delightful the landscape becomes. High mountains give way to gently rolling hills while bare mountain slopes are replaced by densely forested plateaux. This pasture landscape with its beautiful meadows and flowering shrubs is inhabited by the "Sun Elves". Their dwellings, light but strong leafy structures which rise up high into the sky, are mostly situated close to small lakes, clear streams or rivers. The banks of these stretches of waters are home to a large number of animals of every species, which form a natural community with the elves.

The Sun Elves have a great many different characteristics from the Shadow Elves in the north. They have much finer wings, almost like a butterfly, and they wear bright pastel coloured clothes. In contrast to the rune-like ornaments on the robes of the Shadow Elves, the clothes of the Sun Elves are decorated with fine flower patterns or symbols from nature. Due to the warm but never harsh light in this region, the skin of the Sun Elves has a beautiful natural colour. In particular, the fine-featured faces of female elves have a soft, porcelain-like shine. Sun Elves are highly temperamental and take great delight in nature. But they love their horses more than anything else and can barely imagine life without them.

The love of horses is also the aspect which links all elf peoples. Every elf owns at least one horse and looks after it with loving care. However, there is also a very practical reason for this close affinity with horses. Once the sun goes down, elves lose their magic ability to fly. They then need horses to travel quickly from one place to another. Elves can only fly again after their magic power returns when the first rays of sunshine appear in the morning.

Bayala has existed as long as elves can remember and their stories and sagas go far back to an age when the word "battle" still had no meaning. At that time, everyone lived in peaceful harmony with nature - both in the north and the south. But then something happened which was to change life entirely...

The Fateful Night

any years ago when Sera and Surah, the twin sisters, were still babies, Bayala was ruled by a powerful elf king called Baramah. Baramah had three daughters - Sera, Surah and Eyela, the eldest of the sisters.

The elf peoples loved their king, who always had their best interests at heart.

But in the far north of the land lived the elf princess of darkness called Uhara, who was jealous of Baramah. She hated the fact that everyone in the land adored the king. Because she was especially envious of his power, she started to strive after his crown. Her desire became stronger from day to day and she succeeded in casting her evil spell over more and more elves.

Driven by sick desire, she did something which no elf before her had ever dared to do. One dark night she rode to Oracle Mountain, the elves' most holy site. Oracle Mountain was located right in the middle of the land in a region which the elves called "Yala", the lonely country. Situated halfway between the north and south, this region was inhabited by very few elves although the landscape was extremely beautiful. Single high mountains bordered directly on large lowland plains containing small forests. The reason why this region, in spite of its beauty, was so inhospitable was the fog which hung over the countryside every day for many hours after sunrise.

Only Oracle Mountain, the highest mountain in this region, towered up above this fog. During the day Oracle Mountain was guarded by two ancient elves. The task of these two oldest members of the tribe was to protect the holy site against intruders.

But at night even they had to yield to the uncontrollable power of Oracle Mountain and return to their nearby homes. The magical power of the Oracle was too great at night and the impacts for visitors were too unpredictable.

But Uhara was blind with envy, had a firm belief in her own dark abilities and did not want any witnesses to see her when she carried out her plan. She therefore decided to approach the Oracle at night, when all the fog had dispersed.

She had a deep sense of satisfaction when she climbed Oracle Mountain that night. The time had finally come when she hoped to fulfil her most secret dreams.

The Oracle took the form of a round temple-like gallery which was reached via four steps. Sharp pinnacles stretched up into the sky, thus creating the impression of an archway open at the top. Visible in the middle of this gateway was a huge mask-like face, which appeared to be modelled out of light and shadow, and changed its expression with every gust of wind.

Uhara went up to the gallery and fell to her knees. She pleaded and begged for advice. She wanted to know how to overthrow the king and gain power throughout the land. The face of the Oracle changed at rapid intervals, but nothing was heard for a long time. Then finally, when Uhara thought she would never get an answer, the Oracle spoke to her with a deep ominous voice and the whole earth trembled.

"Two sisters, one dark, the other one fair..." the Oracle spoke slowly in riddles. "They are tied by the bonds of love.... break these bonds... then the fate of Bayala will change... and your fate too."

The Oracle spoke no more and an eerie silence settled over the mountain.

The princess of darkness tried to interpret the words. After brooding for a long time, she concluded that the Oracle could only have meant Sera and Surah, the newly born unequal twin daughters of the king.

She rode away that very same night to put her sinister plan into action at the king's splendid elf palace. She rode for many hours until she finally reached her intended destination in the early hours of the morning. She hid the whole day in the woods outside the palace until night-time came again. She used a trick to gain access to the royal chambers where she kidnapped Surah, the younger of the twin sisters. Filled with malicious happiness, she crept outside again and rode the whole night home with the crying baby in her arms.

The dark princess herself had a daughter named Nuray. Over time, Nuray became even darker and more mysterious *than her mother. Since Surah was still a baby when she was kidnapped, she could not remember her background. She was brought up by Uhara and Nuray according to their ways.*

But King Baramah's heart was broken when he discovered that his small daughter had disappeared. Ever since his wife had died giving birth to the twins, his three daughters meant the whole world to him. He sent out his messengers and elf magicians to find Surah, but the hidden power of the princess of darkness was simply too strong. After many years, Baramah was forced to give up the search. He died of grief and despair a short time later. His power had diminished greatly over the years and the kingdom sank into oblivion.

Only Eyela, his eldest daughter, was unable to come to terms with this fate. She continued to cultivate old customs and rites, and remembered the virtues and values her parents had taught her: honesty, boldness and courage. A deep darkness had now returned to the north of the land. The old dark elf princess had interpreted the words of the Oracle in her own way. But this interpretation was wrong and her fate became horribly true. When she realised that her path to the south had been blocked forever by the Oracle, she let out an awful curse which derided the Oracle. The earth began to tremble and heavy pieces of rock fell from her stone palace to the ground. Buried under a large stone, she died on the spot.

Nuray suffered great pain and her heart became a block of ice. She was now heir to Uhara's kingdom and the new powerful elf princess of darkness of the north. She swore to finish what her mother had started. With Surah, she had a powerful weapon in her hand.

The Mysterious Dragon's Head

yela, come with me! I want to show you something." Feya excitedly took hold of her friend's hand and tried to drag her along. "What is it, Feya?" asked Eyela in amazement. "What's so important that you're stopping me from arranging flowers?" Eyela had spent the whole morning picking flowers and now wanted to create some beautiful artistic arrangements. There were only two days to go until the start of the Bannwald Festival, the most important festival of the Sun Elves. There was still a lot of work to be done before the festival and Eyela had no time for anything else. "Don't ask, just come with me," answered Feya impatiently. "It's really important!"

It was a wonderful afternoon and Eyela followed her friend, even though she did not know what could be so important as to interrupt the preparations for the festival. Feya probably only wanted to show her a few flutterlings again. *Flutterlings* are small, colourful, insect-like animals which have eight wings and flit from flower to flower collecting elf nectar. Feya was a dreamer and could spend hours in a meadow watching plants and animals.

"No, there aren't any flutterlings...come on!" Feya was easily able to read the sceptical look in Eyela's eyes.

Feya and Eyela soon came to the edge of the nearby Bannwald forest. This was a sacred place for the Sun Elves since they believed that the deep impenetrable forest contained the souls of their dead ancestors. A large number of elves were busy working in the glade on the southern edge of the forest. Just like Eyela, they were making preparations for the great festival. A short distance away was a small pond containing water lilies. Feya led her friend to the pond.

"Let's sit down underneath this tree, it's a bit cooler here." It was too warm for Feya in the midday sun. The two of them knelt down in a shady spot in the grass. Right in front of them the sun was reflected in the green pond water. "So, what do you want to show me then, dear Feya?" asked Eyela. She was slowly becoming impatient.

"Look into the water." Feya pointed to a shallow area of the pond. The gnarled roots of the old oak tree under which Feya and Eyela were sitting were visible at the bottom of the pond.

"I can only see frogs and dragonflies," replied Eyela in a disappointed voice and looked reproachfully at her friend. There was still much to do before the great festival and she wanted to go home quickly. "No, wait a minute." Feya was annoyed. "Take a closer look. Look really close!" Eyela had rarely seen her friend so serious and determined.

She concentrated hard and looked deep into the water. She couldn't see anything there, or could she?

All of a sudden the water turned blood-red in colour and became very deep. Eyela was so totally engrossed that she couldn't take her eyes off the water. She looked down even deeper into the red water in the pond.

She suddenly heard a familiar voice.

"Eyela, my beloved daughter," said her father from a long way away. It was so long since she had heard the voice of the former King of Bayala, since he had died many years ago. "My father," she cried and her eyes filled with tears. "Where are you? And where are mother and little Surah?"

A long time passed until she heard the voice again. "Eyela, I'm here with our ancestors," replied her father. There was a slight tremble in his voice. "Your mother is also here with me. We are both fine. But Surah.... isn't here." "Where is she then?" called Eyela in despair. It was ages since Eyela had thought about her sister, who disappeared when she was a baby. The pain was too deep.

Eyela's gaze was drawn ever deeper into the red water. There! She could now see her father. He was standing in front of an old grey stone wall and was holding a golden staff in his hand. He looked tired though. His body was bent as though he was carrying a heavy load. He looked at his daughter with kind but sad eyes. "You and your twin sisters are the last members of our royal family," he said. "You, as the oldest, are therefore my successor to the throne of Bayala. But our kingdom is cursed. Our land will never be peaceful until your lost sister has found her peace. The shadows in the north are becoming darker and will also soon reach the south. Do you have strength, Eyela...?" "Strength for what, father?" Eyela asked. The red water in which she was now standing flowed warmly around her feet. "The strength which only a true queen possesses to do the impossible. Something which no elf before you has ever achieved..."

Eyela suddenly saw a dark cloud rising up behind the king. She screamed and wanted to rush to the aid of her father. She could only move very slowly though in the blood-red water. "Father, watch out!" she cried, but the black cloud continued to loom menacingly behind the king. Eyela wanted to help her father and stretched out her left arm towards him. She tried to fly and swim simultaneously, but all her efforts proved in vain on account of the swirling water. She couldn't go any further. Suddenly, when the current appeared to move more slowly, she thought she could see her father very near to her. Although he had almost disappeared in the huge blackness that was starting to envelop him like a dark demon, Eyela bravely reached out for his hand. Baramah now seemed to be really close to her, but his voice sounded thin and distant when he spoke to her again. "Get away from here, Eyela! Get away from this accursed place. But take this with you! It will show you the way..." He tried to push something into her hand but the strong currents separated father and daughter. Eyela didn't give up. With difficulty she moved closer again to the king. And she actually managed to grasp his hand for a moment shortly before he was totally swallowed up by the darkness. She then felt a sharp pain in the palm of her hand. She didn't let go, but clutched even more tightly to the object she could feel in her fist. She was swept away by the red current and her father finally disappeared into the darkness.

Eyela was exhausted and simply let herself be carried along by the current. It seemed as if the red floods surrounding her were continually taking on new shapes. She thought she recognised the face of her friend Feya in the water and that of little Surah before she disappeared. But the faces quickly become blurred again in the currents and other faces appeared. These faces were paler and darker, but Eyela didn't recognise them. They cried out their names with wide open mouths or tried to reach for her with bony hands.

The king's eldest daughter became weaker and weaker. She was scared by everything around her. "I'm finished," she thought, then closed her eyes and lost consciousness.

"Sister!" the call came from nowhere. "Sister!" Somebody was tugging at Eyela's shoulder. "Wake up!" Eyela woke up with a start. The sun was shining in her face.

Where was she? Who had called her? She very slowly came to her senses again. She now recognised Feya and Sera, her younger sister. "Where... where am I?" was the first thing she could say.

"You're here with us at home," she heard Sera say indistinctly from a long way off. "You were sitting at your table and wanted to arrange flowers. You then fell asleep." Eyela now woke up slowly. At home... it was wonderful to hear those words. But what about her experience by the pond and where was her father?

"Feya, my dear, didn't we both just walk to the edge of the forest? You wanted to show me something very important." Eyela looked uncertainly at her friend, but Feya didn't understand Eyela and merely gazed at her with surprise. "I don't think so," she replied. "I was down in the stables with the horses the whole morning and decorated them with flowers for the great festival." Sera took the hand of her older sister. "Oh dear, I think you have a temperature," she said anxiously. "It's not surprising that you tossed and turned so much when you were asleep. You called out to our father when you were dreaming. I will make you a cup of herbal tea. If you drink it slowly, you will soon feel better again."

Sera was very well acquainted with the healing powers of Bayala's plants and people asked her for advice whenever someone was ill.

"I just dreamt everything then," said Eyela in disbelief. "But the dream seemed so real to me. I could swear I spoke to our father." "Father has been dead for many years," replied Sera in a sad voice. "And probably also our twin sister Surah. We shouldn't dig up old stories. What happened, happened and cannot be changed. The fever has made you confused." "I don't know." Eyela didn't like this thought. "You may be right about my fever, but what if Surah isn't really dead? Although I often manage to suppress such thoughts, I am sometimes overcome by dark forebodings. Just imagine she was alive and we stopped looking for her." It was very clear that Sera had the same uneasy thought and tears rolled down her tender cheeks.

"Come, let's go to the others," Feya said after a silence. "The weather outside is marvellous, the flowers are in bloom and the Bannwald Festival will start soon. We should enjoy the day instead of worrying about things we cannot change." "You two can go on your own," replied Eyela in a tired voice. "I want to stay home and drink Sera's tea. Hopefully I will soon feel better again." "If you say so, sister, Feya and I will help the others with their work." Sera was still rather uncertain as to whether she should actually leave her sister alone. "The tea will certainly help you straight away, and you know where to find us if something happens."

After Feya and Sera had gone, Eyela took a long draught from the silver goblet. That felt good! She felt a pleasant warmth spreading through her body. But what was this? Eyela only noticed now that something was clenched in the fist of her left hand. Startled, she opened her fingers wide and a small glittering object fell onto the floor. The prongs of the object had bored deep into the palm of her hand. Eyela only now felt the pain again because a spell had been cast over her by the fever and the after-affects of the dream.

Eyela slowly bent down to pick up the small object. It was the metallic head of a small dragon whose pointed ears and long teeth had pricked her hand, causing the pain. The small face of the dragon looked grimly at its finder. The answer came to Eyela in a flash. "Father!" she cried in a surprised and scared voice. "It wasn't a dream then."

How else did the small dragon's head end up in her hand? Eyela looked more closely at the mysterious head. It was engraved with strange symbols which she didn't recognise. Eyela took an old book out of the cupboard. On the cover it said: *Lost elf languages and mystic symbols*. She sat down at the table with the dragon's head and began to read the book.

The Great Festival

t was already long dark when Eyela put the book aside and lay down wearily on a large velvet sofa decorated with flower ornaments. Her temperature had gone down and Feya had made her a fine meal in the late afternoon. That did Eyela good and she was already feeling much better. She had told neither Feya nor her sister about the dragon's head, for she did not want to worry them. She stretched her legs over the side of the sofa and tried to understand what she had been reading in the book:

A long time ago, the dragons were the most important friends of the elves of Bayala. There were many different races. In the south lived primarily the small, harmless house-dragons, whereas in the north the big, powerful mountain dragons were at home. With the magic of their fire and their overwhelming strength, these mountain dragons helped the

Shadow Elves to build the mighty stone castles that henceforth covered the landscape. The dragons were revered and their image has been eternalised in various ornaments and articles of daily use. But when the great work had been completed, the previously so important helpers were increasingly forgotten and withdrew to their caves, high up in the mountains.

After the land had fallen from grace through Uhara's treachery, and the forests around Oracle Mountain became wrapped in thick fog, mountain dragons came to southern regions only rarely. And when they were seen they were very shy and flew away fast.

The significance of the secret symbols on the little dragon's head that Eyela had received from her father in that mysterious dream, however, she had not been able to find out, even with the help of the book. She continued to brood over the meaning for a while, but then she fell asleep on the sofa.

The two days before the great festival flew by. The preparations were progressing and, as so often with exceptional events, towards the end time was becoming short. But all the Sun Elves were busily involved and were already looking forward to the big event. Eyela had recovered her strength and was working hard and helping with whatever else needed to be done. But she kept finding her thoughts going back to her curious dream and the little dragon's head.

At last! The day of the festival had arrived.

And all the trouble had been worth it. The glade before the Bannwald forest was decorated with thousands of artistic flower garlands. Countless small, filigree silver lights were hanging in the trees and bushes. They consisted of glass balls covered with fine-woven silver thread. In the middle of these balls burned a gentle, violet flame without a wick or wax, just as if lit by a magic hand. These little flames immersed the whole glade and the edge of the forest in an unreal glow.

The light from the silver lamps made the faces of the young elf girls radiate an almost supernatural beauty. An old elf proverb says: *The love of those who fall in love in the night of the Bannwald Festival is eternal.* It was therefore no wonder that Eyela, Sera and Feya were full of excitement and joyful expectation. But not only the elf girls were excited, the young boy elves also wanted to show their best side. At last, on that day the Sun Elves from all over the south of the land gathered at this spot.

In the middle of the glade, an impressive stage with a large, glass dance floor had been erected. When darkness came, many gathered there to dance till the early hours of the morning.

It was a glittering festival. The many lights on the ground and the clear starry sky provided an indescribable backdrop. When the Music Elves picked up their instruments on the large stage and started playing dance music, nobody could sit still. Everyone was happy and laughing. "Oh, I can't go on!" shouted Eyela in a good mood to her friend Feya late in the evening. Both had been dancing happily since darkness had fallen. Now Eyela was out of breath. "I think I need a little break before I carry on dancing." "As you wish," replied Feya. "But I'll stay here. Look at that sweet young elf over there beside the flower column. I can't leave now!" Eyela understood immediately, smiled and left the stage. She walked for a while along the edge of the forest, singing to herself and letting her thoughts roam. Less than three days had passed since she had had that curious dream, and the memory of it came back to her. Since she had acquired the little dragon's head in such a remarkable manner, she had always carried it with her in a pocket of her robe.

She was so lost in her thoughts that she didn't even notice that she was getting further and further away from the glade. Here there were just a few little silver lamps, and it grew darker and darker. Eyela stopped and looked around her. In the distance she could still hear the music and the many voices of the happily celebrating elves. She wanted to lie down on the grass for a while and gaze at the starry night sky. But then she had a terrible fright.

Something was moving behind her! A shadow was approaching. "Who are you?" she called full of fear, and wanted to run away. But somebody held her by the arm. "Stop, stay here!" she heard a young voice with a pleasant melody call. "Don't be afraid. I won't hurt you." She turned round anxiously. Her eyes had meanwhile become a little accustomed to the soft moonlight, and she looked into the eyes of a young elf. "Let me go." Eyela's voice trembled as she pulled her arm away. She wasn't sure what to think of the young elf. "What are you doing here at such a later hour?" she asked, looking at him inquisitively. "Why aren't you with the others?" The young elf laughed. "What about yourself?" he grinned. "After all, you're also walking around away from all the action." "Well... I was lost in thought ...," said Eyela embarrassed, feeling as if she had been caught out. "But that's no reason to frighten me!" "I'm sorry if I frightened you." The young elf seemed sincere. "I really didn't mean to. I was also just walking along the edge of the forest. Sometimes a festival is even nicer if you can observe it from a distance." The young elf looked at Eyela and smiled. "It would appear that two sleepwalkers have met here," he said and grinned challengingly. Now Eyela also had to laugh. There seemed to be no reason to mistrust the young elf. She sat down on the grass, which was still quite warm from the sunshine during the day. "Who are you?" she asked. "Tell me your name." "I'm called Falaroy," he replied. "I live half a day's ride away from here to the south, where the little streams join to form the big river." Eyela knew the area well. It was a very beautiful place, and she had previously made frequent trips with her parents to the area. "But I've never seen you there," said Eyela, looking at Falaroy more closely. But in the darkness she couldn't see much. "You just didn't notice me," replied Falaroy a little offended. "But I know you. You are Eyela, King Baramah's eldest daughter. When I saw you for the first time, you were a little girl and I was a naughty elf boy. But since your father died many years ago, you've never returned to our region." "That's true," Eyela nodded sadly. "The place brings back too many memories of the happy times with my father and my mother. And the elves there have long since forgotten us. The kingdom has fallen into ruins." "Not everyone has forgotten you!" replied Falaroy, suddenly becoming very serious. "Many of us believe that only you can change things, Eyela." Eyela looked up in astonishment. Had her father not said similar words in her dream? Her mistrust returned. She looked at Falaroy severely and then said firmly: "It is no coincidence that I have met you here. You followed me." Falaroy looked to the ground in embarrassment. "That's true," he admitted, "but it's the only way I can talk to you alone. Let's walk along the edge of the forest a little and I'll tell you what brings me to you." Eyela was still unsure whether she could trust Falaroy, but she decided to listen.

The young elf started to tell his story. He spoke of his child-hood, of the golden times of the Sun Elves at the river, and of the creeping changes that have taken place since the fall of the kingdom of Baramah. But before he could get to the real subject of interest, something very unpleasant happened. Smoke suddenly rose from Eyela's robe, and within a flash, flames appeared on the right of her dress, below her hip. Eyela screamed and wanted to put out the fire with her hands. She almost burnt herself. Quick-wittedly, Falaroy threw her to the ground and put out the fire with his cloak before Eyela was in any real danger. Shocked and breathing heavily, they both sat there. It took a while for them to calm down. "What was that?" asked Eyela in a trembling voice. "I... I don't know," stammered Falaroy, who was just as shocked. Only now did he notice that there was still a small, red-glowing object on the ground beside Eyela. "Careful!" he shouted, but the princess had also noticed it. Falaroy wanted to stamp out the embers, but Eyela stopped him. "No, wait!" she shouted, and bent over the glowing object. She now recognised that it was the little dragon's head. Its eyes and the mysterious ornaments were now lit up bright red with glowing heat. This was what had set her robe alight.

But Eyela's fine dress was not the only thing that burned that night. In the far north of the land, Nuray, the dark princess of the Shadow Elves, doubled over in pain. Magic symbols drawn in lines as fine as hair to decorate the skin on her shoulders burned like fire and also appeared to glow red. She attempted to soothe the pain with cold water and damp cloths, but it was to no avail. The burning came from deep inside. She knew it well, for it was the fire of the dragons that always flared up inside her whenever great changes were about to take place.

The Pact with the Dragons

uray had to bear the fire on her skin deep into the night. It drove her to rush restlessly about in her bed chamber. Sometimes the pain was so great that she fell to the floor and writhed in anguish. Then she threw open a window and gasped for air.

Finally, after some excruciating hours, the burning gave way and Nuray fell into a deep, sound sleep.

The clouds hung in the mountains, grey and heavy, when Nuray awoke the next day. The fine symbols on her shoulders did not glow red anymore, but resembled thin, blue blood veins that interwove one another, forming a wavelike pattern.

The princess of darkness rose strenuously from her bed and dragged herself, marked by the agony of the night, into the main chamber of her palace.

Since her mother, Uhara, had died, she had never suffered so much pain from the dragon fire. But Nuray knew exactly what this meant. Her mother had explained it to her when she was still a child. That was when the fine symbols, which had caused her so much pain during the night, had first become visible on her shoulders.

She thus knew that the burning was a sign for impending fateful events, things that would cause profound changes in Bayala and alter the world such that nothing more could be as it had previously been. However, there was no indication of whether these changes would be of a good or evil nature.

The dragon fire which had consumed Nuray went back to an old pact that the dark elf princes of the north had formed with the dragons in some dark, bygone age as they helped in establishing the land of stormy pinnacles and stone palaces. The dragons had made the mountains melt with their flames and hence formed the bizarre structures and houses in which the Shadow Elves now lived.

But the help had its price. The dragons demanded that the dark princes take up a part of the fire in themselves, as an eternal reminder of what they had done for the Shadow Elves. The elf princes of darkness agreed to this pact and each one of them took a sip from a large, golden chalice filled with liquid dragon fire.

As the mountain dragons withdrew more and more into the mountains and the old princes all died or remained childless, the pact nearly sank into oblivion.

Nuray was now the last of the old noble lineage to still bear in herself the flames whose mighty effect was to be felt every now and again. Though since the death of her mother, she had never felt it so strong and threatening as in the past night.

Nuray needed counsel. She was aware of this immediately after she felt a bit better again in the late morning. The dragon fire frightened her on the one hand, though on the other hand, she was excited to discover what it meant. Perhaps it heralded the imminent fulfilment of her mother's dark plans - her desire to subdue and reign over the entire elf kingdom of Bayala. Uhara had passed on this dark idea to her daughter before she died and Nuray viewed it as her duty to fulfil her mother's fateful vision with all available means.

For years now she herself had also striven for control, schemed over new diabolical plans and conjured all secret powers of the land to help her. Yet the shadows to the north had grown darker, and the fog in the middle of the land around Oracle Mountain was often so thick that it was barely possible to pass through. The leaders of her army would never allow a battle at the foot of Oracle Mountain as long as the conditions were so difficult. However, there seemed to be no other way into the Kingdom of Light and even the enchanted elf magic gates had been sealed by the might of the Oracle.

Nuray summoned Ophira. Ophira was her great aunt, and no one was as familiar with the dark arts as she.

"Good morning, my dear Nuray," said Ophira with a smirk, as she entered the living chamber. In the middle of the room, red light shone from a small crater whose round opening was decorated with gold ornaments. "You summoned me. What can I do for you?" "Greetings, Aunt. I am pleased that you so quickly found your way to me," responded Nuray as she kissed her aunt on the cheek.

"I need your counsel," she continued. "The dragon fire burns within me. And it is burning stronger than ever before." Ophira could hardly hide how this news excited her. She rubbed her fingers and looked to the floor. "Now, my dark princess, you know what the fire means?" she then asked in a cool tone, visibly less excited. Nuray nodded and replied in a trembling voice: "Our kingdom is facing upheaval and great changes are imminent. But Ophira, what will happen? That is what I yearn to discover. Please help me to find out, for you are my most loyal servant."

Ophira winced internally at the word *servant,* but stayed outwardly calm and composed. "My niece, let's go down into the vault of the crater, where the treasures of our ancestors lie," she suggested. "Perhaps we shall find something that would give us insight into what lies ahead of us." Nuray felt ill at ease going down into the deep labyrinth-like vault under Crater Mountain, upon which the royal palace was built.

It was a dark and hot place where there was the constant fear of encountering the poor creatures that had sought refuge there. Many years had passed since Nuray had last set foot in these rooms of the palace and even then, only in the highest two levels of the vault.

"Will you follow me or not?" asked Ophira, her impatience increasing. "If I must and if it helps us," responded Nuray reluctantly, setting forth with her aunt.

The vaults under the crater of the royal palace formed a confusing labyrinth of caves that often came together into spacious caverns. Since there were so many of them in levels above and below, it was markedly difficult to find one's bearings. It was very easy to lose one's way. In the halls themselves, the treasures of dark princes from long bygone days were stored. Each prince had his own hall. An old Shadow Elf legend recounted how the spirits of the deceased princes looked after justice and cruelly punished anyone who failed to respect their memory.

Nuray and Ophira knew this and were hence forced to move very carefully and not do anything rash.

Entry into the vault was through an enormous trapdoor in the floor of the entrance hall of the palace. After they had gone down through this door, the two Shadow Elves followed the long, drawn out corridor until they came to the first great hall at the end. Nuray's eyes filled with tears, for it was the hall of her mother. There, Uhara's personal treasures were stored which were no longer required in the palace itself. "Let's hurry up," whispered Nuray. "It saddens me to see these things. We won't find anything here that would help us." Ophira nodded and both of them rushed into the next corridor. This one was clearly less hospitable, since it was much narrower and many spider webs hung from the ceiling in thick strands. Then came the next hall. It was dedicated to Uhara's little brother, whom Nuray had never known, since he had died as a young man. The room, though big, therefore contained few objects.

In this manner, Ophira and Nuray came bit by bit ever deeper into the vault of the crater. The passages became increasingly narrow and inaccessible, and the heat was relentless the further they descended into the crater. The fine, red light grew ever brighter, which Crater Mountain seemed to emit from each of its stony pores.

Maybe two hours had already passed without the two of them having found anything that could give them new insight. Their wings were already entangled with sticky spider webs and their precious robes covered in dust. "We'll have a look at one more hall, but then we should go back," Nuray sighed. "We won't find anything down here that would give us insight into my night-time pains." Ophira was silent and pointed ahead. There was a door to another ancestral hall. They stepped in and looked around. There seemed to be nothing unusual inside. Beautifully decorated precious jugs, vases and pots stood to the left of a large, dark, wooden table. On the other side were two life-size horse statues and at the end of the hall, countless, old robes that were neatly lined up in open, finely constructed wardrobes. Over the years, some of the robes had decayed, but the dry air and constant temperature in the vaults had conserved many of them astonishingly well.

"These things must already be over 300 years old," whispered Nuray, in awe. "Take a look at these horse statues. It's a real pity to leave them lying around down here." She stepped toward the statues to touch the noble works of art. "Stop!" cried Ophira. "For the sake of our ancestors... don't touch anything here or we will be damned!" Shocked, Nuray turned around. How could she have forgotten? Then Ophira raised her hand and said softly: "Be quiet... Can you hear that? What sort of strange sound is that?" Nuray paused and listened. Sure enough, there resounded a peculiar screeching and creaking from afar, with an intermittent deep, penetrating rumbling noise. It was still very quiet, but nevertheless distinct.

Ophira rushed over to Nuray and the horse statues and listened again. "It seems to be coming from this direction," she said and pointed between the two horses in the direction of a big, old wooden shrine, whose doors were closed - the only closed doors in the room. The two elves slowly stepped in its direction and the noises did indeed grow louder. As they then stood before the old shrine, they stopped and listened again. "We have to open the doors to see what is hidden inside," whispered Ophira as she cast a challenging glance at Nuray. "I don't think we are allowed to touch anything," she responded, though her curiosity was at least as great as her aunt's. They hesitated, but then Ophira said: "We have come here to attempt to understand the cause of the dragon fire in you. So let's do it now. Open the door. I will follow you." "You're right," said Nuray, although she felt ill at ease. She took hold of the left door handle, which was decorated with a large, black dragon's head, and turned it...

A sickening, indefinable stench and hot air engulfed them. Nuray pressed her robe against her face to protect herself. They both had to close their eyes for a moment, as a glaring, yellowish-orange light shone from inside the shrine.

When they had accustomed themselves to the light, Ophira was the first to regain her power of speech. "What is that?" she asked, still in wonder. "I would almost say the shrine is a sort of portal." Nuray recognised now as well that there was no back wall to the enormous piece of furniture. A new corridor opened in the back - hot, pungent and full of mysterious noises. "Come on, we must go in," ordered Ophira as she pulled Nuray along through the shrine and into the corridor.

The Mysterious Hall

phira and Nuray went deeper and deeper into the passage. With each step the noises grew louder. Unfortunately, the heat and the stench were getting stronger, so from now on they had to press their robes against their faces in order not to breathe in the bad air. At least the corridor was high, accessible and not clogged with spider webs. "How strange", thought Nuray, "it looks as if someone has passed through here just recently. But who would come to this place?"

The two elves continued for a few minutes along the path through the rocks. Sometimes it went upwards, sometimes steeply downwards. With each step the noise grew louder. Soon the pair came to a heavy stone door with iron fittings. "We're there," whispered Ophira. "The noises are coming from behind this door. Here we will hopefully find out more about the legacy of the dragonfire burning inside you."

She carefully reached for the handle of the door to open it. "Help me," she asked Nuray, "it's too heavy for me alone." With combined strength, they pressed against the massive stone slab, which actually started to move. With a great creaking sound, the door opened.

But when they entered the room, something unexpected happened. Suddenly there was a deathly silence, the light went out and the elves could only see shadows disappearing into the many large and small openings that covered the walls of the room. Nuray thought she saw a wolf-like creature with another creature sitting on its back. But she was not certain she had really seen it, the creature had disappeared so fast. They were now enveloped in darkness, to which they only slowly became accustomed. Gradually they noticed that the room was not completely dark, their eyes just had to get used to a softer light.

Now Nuray and Ophira looked around carefully. They were still under a strong impression of what had happened. What was this mysterious and timid shadowy creature, which had first made such a noise but had then fled before them?

Only now did the Shadow Elves notice that there were lots of small, weak lights in the room. Only the right rear wall of the hall had no cave entrances. Instead, countless little lights glowed across the entire surface of the wall. Nuray now noticed a huge, round, wooden table in the middle of the room, surrounded by at least 40 simple chairs chiselled from stone.

Only now were the elves again able to speak. "Come on, let's go up to the wall with the lights," whispered Nuray. "I'd like to know what this all means." They ran past the wooden table with all the stone chairs to the little lights. They suddenly stopped, agape with astonishment. The entire wall was covered right to the ceiling with little recesses. In each of these countless holes there stood precious little figures made of elf silver and gold. This material was special in that, in contrast with conventional silver and gold, it glowed softly in all the colours of the rainbow as soon as it was in the dark.

The figures depicted quite different things: princes and princesses from former times, magical fable figures, horses and wolves, and, of course, dragons of all types and shapes. "These figures must be priceless," said Ophira, her voice trembling a little. "Yes, they must," agreed Nuray. "Just look at this figure! It's a unicorn with a young rider. They're both beautiful. Do you think I can take them?"

"Are you out of your mind?" Ophira snapped. "We're in the sacred halls of our ancestors. Nothing must be changed here. We'll be lucky to get back to the top safe and sound." Nuray did not like the thought of that very much, but her wish to own at least one of these figures was also very strong. She looked eagerly all over the wall as if she wanted to absorb each individual work of art through her eyes. She suddenly stopped. "Ophira!" she shouted in amazement. "Look, that figure isn't glowing like the others." "True," her aunt agreed, "let's go and take a closer look."

They ran up to the figure. "That's really peculiar," said Ophira astonished and suddenly very excited. "It's an ancient dragon. A creature from a time when no Shadow Elf had a fixed abode in Bayala. I can recognise it by the fine ornamentation on its wings. Those are symbols that today almost nobody can interpret. But the incomprehensible thing is that the figure's head is missing. Somebody must have stolen it. But..." Ophira turned toward Nuray and was shocked. "What's wrong?" Only now had she noticed that the dark elf princess was pressing her hands against the sides of her head and seemed to be screaming in silence with her mouth contorted and wide open.

"Nuray!" she screamed in a state of great excitement. "Nuray! Can you hear me?" Ophira shook her and pulled at her shoulders. Nuray's robe slipped a little, and the burning symbol on her skin came into view. Ophira dragged Nuray away from the figure, but the princess of darkness could no longer walk. And flying was out of the question down here in these narrow vaults.

Without further ado, Ophira gathered all her strength to pick Nuray up and carry her to the exit. Step by step they approached the door, and, fortunately, with every metre they distanced themselves from the wall with the figures, Nuray also seemed to regain her senses. Her aunt managed to carry her to the door and drag her into the corridor through which they had come.

After they had left the hall, the door slammed behind them as if shut by a ghost.

Breathing heavily, Ophira sat on the ground holding the dark princess in her arms.

A dark thought flashed through her mind. Was she not Nuray's last true relative and heir? What would happen if Nuray now just simply disappeared mysteriously? Ophira could not suppress a wicked smile, for she saw herself for a moment as the ruler of the Shadow Elves in the chambers of the palace.

But Nuray had meanwhile fully recovered. "What ... what happened?" she stammered, a confused expression on her face. "I had the feeling that I was standing in a sea of flames and burning!"

Ophira was only able to suppress her vision with difficulty. "What do you mean?" she asked distractedly. "Oh yes!" she then called out. "The fire took hold of you when you saw the little dragon without its head. I think that we have come a lot closer to finding the solution to what happened last night and what might happen in future. The dragon's head - where could it be? I think that if we find the answer to that, we'll be very close to the truth! But let us now go back. We've got a long way before us and you are still weak. I can't possible carry you the whole way. Or should I leave you here and fetch help?" "No!" shouted Nuray. "No way! I'm strong enough to walk. You just need to support me a little from time to time. Come on, let's go."

Nuray stood up, still a little unsteady. Ophira looked her over from the side, but then quickly came to her assistance and supported her.

They slowly made their way back the way they had come. Curiously, with every step they moved away from the hall, the scratching and screeching noises seemed to become louder.

Finally, it was just a few more metres to the hall with the shrine through which they had passed. The direct path from there was no longer very far, so they should soon be back at the top.

Then suddenly a large, black figure arose before them, exactly at the moment they were about to go through the shrine door. Nuray and Ophira had a terrible fright. "Who are you?" Nuray called out in great fear. "Who dares to stand in the way of the dark princess of the Shadow Elves?" Loud laughter rang out, echoing like thunder in the large chamber. "It is I, Turag, standing in your path." And again his loud laughter resounded.

Surah and Shadow Rock

Turag, it's you!" cried Nuray full of joy when she finally recognised the tall black-clad elf, the commander of her kingdom's army. "Greetings, my princess of darkness," Turag replied and laughed again. He then bowed down before Ophira and greeted her as well. "I heard you had gone down into the vaults and thought you might need some help," he continued. "This is not a nice place to stay very long. The spirits of the past rule here." Nuray and Ophira exchanged a knowing look. "The spirits of the past aren't the only ones who rule here", thought Ophira to herself and the strange creatures from the hall of figures came to mind again.

"You've come at just the right time, Turag," said Nuray with relief and a small smile on her lips. "I really feel rather weak. We spent far too long in the narrow vaults and I'm terribly thirsty." Turag supported the dark princess with his strong arms.

They were now able to move much more quickly. Nuray, Ophira and Turag soon reached the large trapdoor in the entrance hall, through which they had gone into the cellar that morning. Nuray and Ophira heaved a great sigh of relief when the door in the floor was shut behind them.

𝒟usk was slowly falling, and outside the gates of the palace, thick black clouds of mist were swirling down into the valley from the mountains.

"That's strange," said Nuray in a surprised voice. "We didn't spend too much time in the halls of our ancestors. It can't be any later than afternoon." "Didn't you know that time in the deepest vaults of the palace has no meaning?" asked Turag with astonishment. "Demons and spirits rule the roost down there. But you were lucky. The spirits were kind to you. Some Shadow Elves went down there in the past and were never seen again." Nuray shuddered at the thought. Her mother had only ever taken her into the topmost vaulted halls and, even as a child, Nuray had great respect for the ancestral halls and the age-old treasures inside.

When Uhara died many years ago, Nuray wanted nothing more to do with the caves and the halls. But then she remembered that her mother had warned her once not to go too deep into the passageways.

"Ophira, did you know of this danger?" Nuray asked her aunt, "I had no idea it was so dangerous." She looked Ophira up and down. "Yes, my dear niece, I know these stories," replied Ophira. "But I didn't want to make you too anxious, because there's no cause to worry. Look," she raised her right hand and pointed to a bracelet on her wrist. The bracelet looked like two closely intertwined snakes. The two heads of the snakes were studded with precious stones and formed the catch of the elaborately designed piece of jewellery. The imitation poisonous teeth of the snakes bit firmly into one another. "Your mother gave me this bracelet sometime in the past," she explained. "Whenever I am with you, it protects you against evil demons. But, unfortunately, you can never wear the bracelet yourself, as its magic would then not work."

Nuray looked very closely at the magic bracelet. She also then remembered that Ophira had always accompanied her when she went into the vaults a few times after her mother's death. "But why did you never tell me about this?" asked Nuray in a surprised voice. Ophira gently stroked her hair and said: "You are carrying enough burdens as the heir to the Shadow Kingdom and I didn't want to worry you. Your memories of your mother are also very painful. But times have now changed! The dragon fire is burning in you again and great changes are imminent. It's now time to talk about the past and fulfil the legacy of your mother."

Nuray stole a glance at Turag as if she wanted to indicate to Ophira that they shouldn't talk about such matters in the presence of her army commander. But Turag did not appear to be interested. He was talking and joking with an elf who had come running up with a glass containing silver water. Silver water was only found in the mountain springs in the high north and was well-known for its revitalising effects.

When Nuray and Ophira stopped talking, Turag turned to them again and gave the dark princess the water to drink. "Here, my lady," he said, bowing down before her. "You said you were very thirsty." "Thank-you, Turag," replied Nuray with relief. She quickly swallowed some of the silver water. The water did her some good and she felt her strength return with each sip of the elves' drink.

Ophira, however, glanced sideways at Turag with suspicion. "How did he know about the secrets of the vaulted cellar?"

she thought to herself. "And how was he simply able to climb down and find us without falling victim to the curse of the spirits?" With a penetrating look, she tried to find some hint of the secret she suspected Turag was hiding. But then she turned round abruptly with a rather tired smile on her face and said:

"Well then, it was a hard day. I'm tired and now wish to go to my chamber. Do you still need me, my dear niece?" "No, Ophira," replied Nuray. "Thank you very much for your help." Ophira gave the two of them a short nod and left.

Turag looked at Nuray with a serious expression on his face. "It's good that we're alone now, my princess," he whispered and then looked around as if he was afraid of being overheard. "There's something you really must see!" Nuray was astonished, but Turag seemed so serious and determined that she simply followed him, despite her fatigue, without saying a word.

The corridor led into the upper rooms of the palace, where guests were normally accommodated. There was a glass door on the rear wall of a very large and beautifully decorated room. When the door was opened, it led directly outside.

A barren stony plateau offered a view of the entire Shadow Kingdom of the north. But there was something much more obvious: At the end of this rocky plateau, not far from a yawning abyss, stood an impressive building. Although it was slightly remote, it obviously still belonged to the palace because it was constructed in exactly the same way as the other part of the building.

This place had a very special meaning for the elves of the north. They called the building *Shadow Rock*. It was the oldest structure built by dragons and was therefore regarded as a sacred place. Shadow Rock rose up into the sky. It was regarded as a very safe building because it defied all the elements on account of its stone walls burnt by the fire of dragons. It was therefore no coincidence that the palace's most thoroughbred horses were kept there. Celebrations were held and new alliances were forged in this place. Only the most important guests were allowed to live there for the duration of their stay and enjoy the breathtaking view.

The elves had built a safety wall behind Shadow Rock in order to prevent anyone from falling down into the abyss when it was dark.

It was now dark when Turag and Nuray approached Shadow Rock. Nuray saw straightaway that a small light was burning in the top, open storey of the building.

"What is that?" she whispered. "Nobody in my palace is permitted to be here at this time without my permission!" Turag and Nuray carefully crept closer. The dark princess now recognised a slim figure holding the small light in her hands. "Who is it?" she whispered again and gave Turag a questioning look. "Surah," he replied very quickly in a barely audible voice. *Surah...* the name flashed through Nuray's mind. She could still easily remember their childhood together when she always had to share her mother with Surah, although the kidnapped daughter of King Baramah was not really her daughter. She had to swear several times to her mother that she would never speak to Surah about her real origins, as otherwise the Shadow Kingdom would be doomed. Nuray kept this promise, although she was often consumed by jealousy.

Surah had withdrawn into herself since the death of Uhara. Although she still lived in the palace, she hardly ever left her chambers. Nuray spoke very rarely to her and only then when it was absolutely necessary. But sometimes in the night when everyone was asleep, she heard Surah walking restlessly through the corridors of the palace, almost as if she was looking for something.

Turag and Nuray crept a bit closer. They could now see Surah's enraptured face. Her half-closed eyes were lit by the small light. Nuray now also realised that the light wasn't normal. She had to look even more closely - was it possible? The light appeared to resemble a small figure. From a distance it looked like a dragon. But a dragon without a head! That couldn't possibly be the figure which she herself had seen in the deep vaults and had caused her so much pain.

Surah's whole body now started to tremble slightly. She incessantly stammered soft words which Nuray couldn't understand. But then something happened which the princess of darkness had never seen before. Out of the torso of the small dragon flowed a white mist which immediately wrapped itself around Surah's body and wings like a magic spell. Surah trembled more and more, and the mist became even thicker. She only mumbled incomprehensible and incoherent words. The mist gushing out of the small dragon figure was now so thick that Surah was barely visible.

All of a sudden there was a flash of lightning and a roll of thunder was heard in the distance. A light breeze sprung up and quickly turned into a strong gale which blew away the mist. But Surah also disappeared with the mist as if she had dissolved into thin air. Only the small figure was left lying on the ground, and its light slowly started to fade.

Nuray caught her breath. "Where is she?" hissed Nuray to Turag. "She can't just have disappeared!" "It seems she has," replied Turag. "But the strange thing is that she will be back here again tomorrow when the whole spectacle will be repeated." "Does that mean she does this every evening?" asked Nuray, clearly annoyed. Turag nodded. "Why wasn't I told about this much earlier?" shouted Nuray, now really angry. "Does my aunt know what happens here?" Turag shook his head. "I've never told her," he replied in a firm voice. "And why are you shouting so loud at me, dark princess?" His voice suddenly sounded loud and threatening. "Ask Surah yourself what she's doing here!"

Nuray gave Turag an angry look and then turned around and ran away. She would get to the bottom of this matter in the morning, because one thing was certain: Surah posed a danger to her and the entire kingdom. This realisation pulsed through her veins.

Only when Nuray was back in her chambers did she suddenly become aware that, unlike the first encounter in the hall of figures, she didn't feel that indescribable pain when she looked at the small headless figure. She brooded over this for a long time, wondering whether it was due to the streaming mist or an entirely different reason.

But Nuray wasn't the only one still awake. Ophira hadn't gone to sleep yet. Her feigned tiredness had only been a pretext to leave Turag and Nuray, and forge her own plans. Shortly before she had left Turag and Nuray alone, she had noticed something rather strange. A bracelet appeared to be hidden underneath the sleeve on Turag's left forearm. She was only able to look at it for a fraction of a second, at precisely the moment when Turag reached for Nuray's water glass and his sleeve had slipped up slightly. It seemed to her that he, too, was wearing a snake bracelet which looked exactly like her own - a bracelet which was reserved only for the dark princes and which she herself had stolen from Uhara's room straight after her death.

In the Kingdom of Mist

urah came to her senses. Everything around her seemed to be wrapped in cotton wool. The white mist enveloping her was so dense that it seemed she could touch it, but it was also so opaque that she could no longer see her own feet. Surah stretched out her arms in front of her as if she was looking for something. She didn't know whether she was actually standing on the ground or floating in the air because the mist was so thick that it absorbed and destroyed any perception of time and space. Surah tried to move, run or fly in order to escape from the stiff white mantle all around her. But she had the feeling that she couldn't actually move and she had no idea where she wanted to go.

She yelled out in despair. Surah cried aimlessly into the distance because she had nobody to call out to.

Ever since the death of Uhara, whom she thought to be her mother, Surah had felt alienated, exactly as if half of her had been lost. Although she attributed this to Uhara's death, she was increasingly overcome by doubts as to whether another secret might not be the reason for her painful longing.

In spite of all the dangers, her loneliness had driven her a long time ago down into the deepest vaults beneath the palace - the very place where Nuray and Ophira had also been.

Surah wasn't aware of the dangers lying in wait for her down there. She also had no idea that she was really Baramah's daughter and that the demonic magic had no power over her in the vaults because of her royal ancestry.

In the ancestral hall Surah had also discovered the figures which had almost proved Nuray's undoing. She made an astonishing discovery when she looked more closely at the small works of art. All the figures - large and small, dragons and kings - were basically small vessels made of glittering elf silver and elf gold. The head of the figures acted as a lid which, when opened, released the liquid contents of the particular figure. Surah had taken some of the small figures into her chamber where she discovered the secret of the mist which was produced from the liquid inside the figures. She experienced how the mist took hold of her, joined together with her body, made her lose consciousness and transported her to a place where everything seemed to suffocate in the mist.

From now on, Surah retreated in the evening into Shadow Rock as a place of transformation. She felt totally safe there, even though she was very afraid of what would happen and was often full of despair. She had to go on this journey into the mist time and time again because she believed that only then would she learn something about herself and her destiny.

Surah bent her body to shake off the white mist, but it seemed to embrace her more firmly than ever. Then all of a sudden, she felt the ground giving way beneath her feet. She thought she was falling. The white mist around her drifted past and was replaced by pitch-black darkness. Surah tried to fly, but her wings seemed to be totally powerless. Lights rushed past her. She then seemed to be caught in a picture again: she had the feeling she was surrounded by an impenetrable forest containing huge trees. She saw elves between the trees, but they appeared transparent and fragile, and shyly hid themselves behind the mighty tree trunks as soon as they spotted Surah.

She was then pulled out again from the trees high up into the sky. Wisps of clouds drifted past her and it turned icily cold. The crystal-clear night sky seemed to flow through her body. Suddenly she felt ground beneath her feet again. For a moment she thought she could see the almighty Elf Oracle in the darkness. Was she on Oracle Mountain? How on earth had she got there? But then everything went fuzzy once more and she started falling again. Surah now felt she was falling out of the sky. She saw shining stars on the left and right, and the highest mountains of the Shadow Kingdom appeared below her. She fell and fell... the steep rock walls of the high mountains rushed past her until it suddenly became dark again. A reddish light flickered constantly. Surah's only thought was that a powerful maelstrom was pushing her through dark cave passages. Wild creatures seemed to be laughing at her and hands with sharp claws reached out to her. The maelstrom became even stronger. Just before she lost consciousness again, Surah saw a wall containing a large number of small lights in a room which was occupied by countless demonic beings.

When she awoke, she was lying bathed in sweat on her bed and had difficulty breathing. She couldn't explain what had happened to her. On the other occasions when she travelled into the Kingdom of Mist she had never come out again. She had always been caught in the white mist until she came round again in her room. But this time she managed to break free, even though what happened afterwards was like a trip through hell.

Nevertheless, Surah felt relieved. For the first time since the death of Uhara she knew she had come a step closer to finding out the truth. Secure in this knowledge, she fell asleep.

$\mathcal{F}$ar way from the palace of the Shadow Elves in the kingdom of the Sun Elves, Sera woke up in her bed with a start. What was that? She thought she had heard a cry. Had someone called out to her? She listened carefully, but everything around her was calm and still. She quickly got out of bed and ran to the window. The stars were shining in the night sky and spread a silvery sheen over the fields and trees. There was nothing untoward here. A shooting star fell from the sky and Sera quickly closed her eyes in order to make a wish. She then went back to bed. But although everything seemed quiet outside, Sera still spent a restless night.

Sera got up very early the next day. It was the third morning after the great Bannwald Festival and she had arranged to meet her sister Eyela and her friend Feya in *Summergreen House*.

This house was a place where the Sun Elves loved to meet one another. Everyone felt at home there because there was always a happy atmosphere. Young elves played games or rode on the swings in front of the house. Music was playing and anyone wanting to could dance. However, Sera liked the horses there best of all. She loved horses more than anything and even during the day when she could fly, she often preferred to ride one.

But there was a serious reason today for meeting at this magical place. Everyone was still afraid of the danger to which Eyela had been exposed on the night of the Bannwald Festival when her dress went up in flames. Eyela had said that she wanted to get to the bottom of this strange event after the clearing-up work had finished. Falaroy, who had seen this for himself and extinguished the fire with great presence of mind, had remained. He, too, wanted to help uncover the secret. Deep in his heart, he also hoped that Eyela would remember his words and take heed of them. He believed that she should think about her royal origins because only she could re-establish the lost kingdom and reunite the whole of Bayala. Falaroy was quite certain of this.

Sera still felt rather tired that morning when she stood combing her hair in front of the mirror. She plaited a few flowers in her hair and pulled on a light summer dress. She had also noticed that Falaroy was a good-looking, brave young elf and, even though she hated to admit it, she wanted him to like her. She sprayed some blossom nectar in her hair and then flew away.

When she arrived at Summergreen House, the others were already waiting for her. Sera was always the last to arrive and Feya couldn't help making some teasing remarks.

Eyela, Sera, Feya and Falaroy then sat down at a table and started talking with one another. In the middle of the table was the small dragon's head whose glowing had set Eyela's robe on fire. Sera and Feya were amazed when Eyela related how she had found the dragon's head after her strange dream. Sera glanced at her sister reproachfully and said: "You should have told us all this much sooner. Who knows what danger you may have been in."

Eyela again had to relate in detail what had happened that night when her robe had caught fire. They all then fell silent for a while and Feya looked closely at the small dragon's head. This simple object had such an enormous effect! She could hardly credit it. She gave the others a questioning look and then said: "Eyela, why don't you simply throw the head away or bury it? It's ugly and it's only caused you trouble since you found it." Eyela shook her head. "No, Feya," she replied, "I received the dragon's head when I dreamt about my father. I can't just throw it away." Sera gave her sister a sceptical sideways glance. "You found the dragon's head when you had a temperature and weren't thinking straight," she cautioned. "How do you know that someone else didn't just slip it to you? There may be a curse on it!" Feya nodded in agreement, but Falaroy just stared at the floor. "No," he then said, "that's not right. There must be a secret behind all this, and I have a feeling that it is an important secret." Eyela was grateful that Falaroy took her seriously and said: "Perhaps I was in a feverish delirium, but what I saw and experienced in the dream was so real that I can still talk about it any time. Father was standing before me, Sera, believe me!" Sera nodded pensively and thought again about her last sleepless night. "I think we should really try and find the key to the secret," she then said, "who knows what else it will reveal to us. "What if we again followed the path which Eyela took that night?" suggested Falaroy. "Let's see whether or not the same thing will happen again. But we must then try to interpret the signs." This thought made Eyela very uneasy. "I won't carry the head with me though. That's too dangerous for me," she observed.

"Of course not," said Falaroy in a reassuring voice, "we will place the head in a fireproof elf glass and I will carry it so that we can see it at all times." "Alright," replied Eyela after some hesitation, "let's do it then. In the early afternoon we'll meet at the place where the large stage for the Bannwald Festival recently stood."

The Tree Gateway

Some time later, Eyela, Sera, Feya and Falaroy stood at the edge of the forest where the festively illuminated stage had been until recently and wonderful elf music could be heard. However, the Festival had finished long ago.

"It must have been over there!" said Eyela pointing to a small clump of trees. "I started running from there - keeping to the edge of the forest. Come with me."

Falaroy had placed the small dragon's head in a receptacle made of elf glass and was carrying it in front of him in full view of everyone. Elf glass was a very special material. Only a few specialists could work with it. It was unbreakable and not even a red-hot fire could melt it. It only lost its special characteristics for a short while on nights when there was a full moon. On these occasions it could be worked just like normal glass.

The four elves walked slowly along the path at the edge of the forest. It was a marvellous summer's day and Feya was rather sad that she simply couldn't fly over the meadows, pick flowers and enjoy the sunset later at the large pond. But Eyela and Sera were her best friends and she certainly didn't want to leave them in the lurch. She continually stole glances at Falaroy. "It's really sweet to see him carrying the receptacle containing this stupid dragon's head, as if it were a precious object," she thought. Sera's glance met hers. Feya realised at once that Sera had similar thoughts and both of them giggled. Falaroy turned round in irritation. "Is there something wrong?" he asked uncertainly. "Of course not," replied Sera with a grin. "Everything's fine. We... we were just thinking about a friend who looked after Feya very well during the Bannwald Festival," she said after searching for a simple excuse for her silly giggling. "Yes, that's right," confirmed Feya. "He was simply charming." "Well, then...," stammered Falaroy and turned round again. Eyela looked reproachfully at Sera and Feya because of course she knew exactly what the two of them had been thinking. But she, too, was forced to suppress a grin because she saw precisely the same appealing characteristics in Falaroy as her sister and her friend.

The four elves carried on along the edge of the forest for a while without anything untoward happening. They talked a lot, made jokes and had almost forgotten there was a serious reason for coming this way. The trees at the edge of the forest were so dense and tall that hardly any sunlight filtered through. Anyone looking slightly more closely through the trees into the interior of the forest could soon only see darkness, which made the Bannwald forest seem so impassable. No Sun Elf would ever think about going into the Bannwald forest. Firstly because it was the sacred place of their dead ancestors and secondly, because there was no reason to exchange the sunlight in southern Bayala for this darkness.

Eyela slowed down slightly since the group was now approaching the place where her robe had gone up in flames. She looked all around her uncertainly, but nothing here appeared to be any different from what they had seen along the way. Everyone was silent and started feeling a strange tension which was out of place on this beautiful summer's day.

"Look here!" cried Falaroy. He stopped and raised a warning hand. Everyone looked spellbound at the glass receptacle containing the small dragon's head. "Can you see it?" he whispered in an excited voice. "The strange ornaments are turning red. It almost looks as if blood is flowing through these finely patterned veins." Eyela took a step backwards. The memories of her strange dream and the flames came back strongly to her and made her feel afraid.

Everyone just carried on walking slowly. With every step they took, the red colour increased in strength and also engulfed the rest of the dragon's head.

"It must have been here," said Eyela shortly afterwards. "I'm almost certain. What do you think, Falaroy?" But Falaroy didn't reply. He just stared entranced at the glass. The small dragon's head had now turned completely red and appeared to be glowing. Falaroy clung desperately to the receptacle. "The glass is getting hot!" he cried out suddenly. "That's not possible! It's elf glass!"

Everyone stared in bewilderment at the glowing head. It actually seemed as if some marks were starting to appear on the inside wall of the container due to the heat.

Falaroy quickly put the glass down on the ground because it was too hot to hold in his hands. All of a sudden the elves heard loud cracks and groans coming right from the edge of the forest. "Just look!" exclaimed Eyela. "The trees are moving!" Some of the very large trees at the edge of the forest actually bent down and formed an arch. "What does that mean?" whispered Sera in a very scared voice. The sky above the Bannwald forest had now turned dark and heavy thunder clouds were gathering. "It almost looks like a gateway," said Feya in a trembling voice. "The trees are opening up a path into the interior of the forest." "But we're not allowed to go in there!" shouted Eyela. "It's far too dangerous. If there..." "Just look!" Falaroy interrupted. "There on the ground... the fire track!" A fine burning track now snaked from the glowing dragon's head towards the bent trees. Falaroy bent down and carefully touched the glass to see whether it was still as hot as before. To his astonishment, it had cooled down slightly as if the heat had flowed out. He could therefore pick it up again.

"Let's follow the track to the edge of the forest," he suggested. "Nothing can happen to us." The others agreed and they all slowly followed the burning track. A storm was now brewing above the trees. The first clouds became thicker and a flash of lightning lit up the sky. "Let's get away from here!" cried Sera in great fear. "I think a storm is coming!" "You're right. Perhaps it would be better if we went," said Falaroy. But just when the four elves were about to leave, a bolt of lightning struck a small tree right in front of them and threw them to the ground. More and more bolts of lightning lit up the sky, continually striking into the earth. "We can't get away from here!" exclaimed Falaroy. "We have to find a safe place as quickly as possible. Come on, let's run into the forest. Perhaps there's a cave or a rock overhang there where we can shelter." The first heavy drops of rain started falling. This was soon followed by a thundershower, the likes of which the four elves had never seen before. They quickly ran towards the edge of the forest to look for shelter.

Cyela was the first one to run through underneath the bent trees. The others followed right behind her. And suddenly... everything was quiet! The four elves looked around and saw the trees straightening up again. Shortly afterwards, the trees were standing tall and close together again as if nothing had happened. "That's uncanny," whispered Feya in a trembling voice. "Let's get away from here as quickly as possible." But when the elves tried to leave the forest where they had come in, they couldn't get out. Behind the first trees they saw other tall trees which in turn were followed by even taller trees. It seemed as if the elves were no longer at the edge of the forest, but had got lost. "There must be a way out somewhere!" shouted Sera in despair. "We only just came in." Compared with the loud thunderstorm, the sudden stillness in the forest now appeared to the elves to be even more eerie.

"Look there," said Falaroy pointing to the small dragon's head again. "The object is no longer glowing, it's only shining." Everyone stared in disbelief at the glass. It was really true. "What does that mean?" asked Eyela, although she knew that none of them could answer her question. "I don't know, unfortunately," replied Falaroy. "But at least we have some light. Otherwise it would be really dark here." This only proved a small consolation to Feya. All she could see was tall trees close together. The dense treetops didn't let any rays of sunshine through. "That's no help at all." Eyela was the first to regain her composure. "Staying here won't get us any further. Come on, let's look for a way out. After all, it can't be very far." "Eyela's right," said Falaroy. "We have to do something. We can't count on any help here. Let's go in this direction." Falaroy pointed forward resolutely. In truth, he had no idea in which direction they should go, he only wanted to raise the girls' spirits.

The Pyramid in the Forest

alaroy proceeded purposefully and Eyela, Feya and Sera followed him. The forest was so dense they could hardly get through, and hardly any light penetrated the treetops to the ground. Even the little dragon's head glowed only very weakly and Falaroy kept stumbling in the darkness.

While the elves tried to clear their way through the forest, Falaroy made an interesting observation: the little head was not always glowing with the same strength. Sometimes the soft glow became weaker, and then, upon a change of direction, it again became more intensive. The longer the elves wandered through the forest, the more this fascinated Falaroy. "Eyela, Sera, Feya, look here," he turned to the others and told them of his observation. "The dragon's head's glow is now getting stronger again. But what's the reason?

Let's just go in the opposite direction." Falaroy and the elf girls turned round and slowly went back the way they had come. "What do you want to show us, Falaroy?" asked Eyela, but the young elf was just staring at the glass. "Look!" he exclaimed, "the glow immediately becomes weaker when we go in the wrong direction. I get the feeling the dragon's head wants to guide us through the forest." "You mean that little thing is a guiding light showing us the way?" Feya asked curiously, suddenly very attentive. She didn't feel at all at ease in the forest, and hoped to get back out into the open as soon as possible.

Guiding lights were of great significance in the mythical world of Bayala, and they existed in the most varied forms. Almost every lord or prince in the land had at least one. Their use was very difficult, as you could never tell whether they were guiding you to your desired destination or just leading you astray. For a long time, guiding lights had therefore hardly been any longer in use, but were now merely a symbol of wealth and power.

"Maybe the little dragon's head is a guiding light," replied Falaroy. He too knew the old stories and knew about the appeal, but also the dangers, of these lights. "Whatever the case," Eyela commented, "we haven't any choice but to follow it, because it's our only source of light, and without light we are lost here in the Bannwald forest." "What a pity that the forest is so dense," Sera now remarked. "If there were a little more daylight, we might be able to fly. Then we'd soon be up through the trees and out in the open." "That doesn't help us much at the moment," said Falaroy impatiently. "We should be glad to have any light at all, and it might still lead us to the right place. Come, let's go on." Eyela nodded and the three girls followed Falaroy and the light in silence.

The elves struggled on through the forest. Almost insuperable obstacles appeared in their path. Broken branches or dense, mistletoe-like plants made their progress almost impossible. Sometimes the ground was damp and marshy, and then again almost impassable on account of large rocks. What was much more unpleasant, however, was the strange noises, which were sometimes clear and then muffled. Like a constant whispering, countless voices penetrated the elves' ears, yet it was impossible to understand a single word. "Those are certainly the voices of our dead ancestors," whispered Feya reverentially with a shudder. "They are probably trying to warn us not to go deeper into the forest." "No," replied Eyela decisively, "it's only the gentle rustling of the leaves." She wanted to put Feya's mind at rest, but the slight trembling in her voice revealed that she too did not feel at ease.

"I'm so hungry. Aren't you too?" Sera remarked. The others nodded. Meanwhile they were all hungry and tired, but there was no end to their journey in sight. They all knew that it might be ages before they were out of the forest, if there was any escape at all. Dispirited and gloomy, they continued on their way.

"Look there!" shouted Falaroy after a long period of silence when the light of the dragon's head was again getting brighter. They all strained to look ahead and tried to see in the dark. But what was this? Between the trees they saw a large shadow, like a narrow pyramid, rising between the trees up to the highest treetops. The elves now started to run faster to see what the mysterious structure signified, and with each step the silhouette became clearer. Shortly after, they were standing before a huge, pyramid-like building that had withstood the wildly growing plants here in the middle of the forest. The pyramid consisted of a single, pointed block of stone. On the three side walls, various ornaments and symbols were engraved in the stone. The elves were amazed. "It's strange that all the climbing plants and creepers here in the forest haven't overgrown everything," Eyela remarked. And also the moss and fungus seemed not to be growing on the walls. "Look!" exclaimed Feya, "on this side there's a door through which we might be able to get inside the pyramid."

The others ran over to Feya and there was indeed a bronze handle on the wall. The door itself was hardly recognisable, as it was made from the same stone as the entire pyramid. Eyela pointed to the ornaments engraved in the stone and said with a quivering voice: "These are the symbols of our old kingdom. My father Baramah had these symbols embroidered on his golden king's robe that he wore on festive occasions. Also in our family heritage book there are such symbols stamped on the first pages." Sera was astonished, because she naturally also knew the old symbols of her father.

"I think we should open the door and go inside," Falaroy suggested. "Outside in the forest we are lost and don't know which way to go." "You're probably right," Eyela agreed. "Inside the pyramid we'll hopefully find a place where we can sleep a little. When we've rested, we might find a solution as to how to get away from here. I just hope it's not dangerous in there." She resolutely gripped the handle and wanted to pull hard to open the door. But as soon as her delicate hand touched the door, it opened. They couldn't see anything inside, it was almost completely dark.

"I'll lead the way," said Falaroy bravely. "After all, I've got the little dragon light, and now it's glowing brighter than ever." So the four elves entered the stone pyramid.

And then something unexpected happened. The moment Falaroy, Eyela, Feya and Sera passed through the door, a bright, warm light suddenly illuminated the pyramid, and it was impossible to see where the light was coming from. Also, the room seemed much bigger inside than expected from the outside. But the most astonishing thing was that for the four elves all tiredness, hunger and thirst seemed to vanish. Falaroy looked at Eyela in amazement. "What does it mean?" he asked. "This is a strange kind of magic." Eyela was about to say something, when the stone door closed with a crash behind them. Falaroy and the elf girls turned with a start, but now, where just before there had been an open door, there was just a smooth, stone wall.

"How will we ever get out of here!" shouted Feya in terror. "We're locked in." Sera tried to calm her friend. "Be glad that it's now light and we're no longer hungry. We'll find a way out. Besides... have you noticed that the room seems to be growing slowly? From outside, the pyramid seemed smaller than it now appears from the inside." "That's true," Eyela agreed. "I noticed that too. And look over there on the wall. I think that's a little fountain with silver water." Otherwise the room seemed to be almost empty, apart from one thing that couldn't be missed: in the middle of the room there was a life-sized, very simple dragon figure with a silver body standing on its strong legs. "Just look!" said Falaroy. "The little dragon's head is now glowing brightly. You'd almost think it's about to start burning." The others looked at the object curiously. "Do you think it wanted to guide us precisely to this place?" asked Falaroy. "At least, there's a dragon figure here too, even if to my taste it looks a little ugly." "It's not that ugly," Feya replied. "It just hasn't got any ornaments or other adornments. But if I'm not mistaken, the material from which the body is made is pure elf silver." The four stepped closer to examine the dragon more closely. Only now did they notice that a fine mist was coming out of its silver mouth, rising and thus evidently creating the light in the room. "Look!" said Eyela, "there's a fine seam around the dragon's neck. The head is apparently not connected to the body, but just placed on it." "You're right," agreed Falaroy. "What a strange coincidence. A little dragon's head leads us to a place where there's a silver dragon figure whose head is also not connected to its body. No, that can't be a coincidence." "I don't think so either," Eyela was also sure. "My father gave me the little dragon's head that has now led us to this pyramid. The door to the pyramid is decorated with the holy symbols of our kingdom, and here inside we find this dragon. I don't know about you, but I feel very safe here, even happy. It almost seems as if it's the wish of my dead father for us to find this place." Sera nodded, for she felt the same.

However, Feya was still unable to hide her unease. Falaroy too felt great trepidation, even if he was reluctant to admit it to the elf girls. "Maybe you two feel so good as it's a secret place of your old kingdom," Falaroy remarked, "and you are the only living ancestors. Just think, the door opened at the mere touch of your hand, Eyela. Feya and I are perhaps less welcome here, as no royal blood flows through our veins."

Eyela nodded slowly. "You may be right, Falaroy," she agreed with her companion. "But we're all in the same boat now, and I just want us all to get away from this place and out of the forest together." This idea seemed to calm Feya a little. "But what should we do?" she asked uneasily, looking around nervously, for the room still seemed to be expanding slowly. "If only I knew," Eyela pondered. "But I believe that the solution has something to do with this dragon." Falaroy was now examining more closely the seam separating the dragon's head from the body. "Maybe we should try to have a look inside the dragon's body," he suggested. "After all, fine mist is coming out of the mouth, which would suggest that there is something inside the large figure." "And if it's too dangerous?" Sera demurred. "After all, we don't know what to expect."

The four elves discussed things a while longer, but no-one came up with a better idea.
"Alright, then, we'll do it," Eyela finally decided. "We'll look inside the dragon figure."
A short time later, the four elves were standing before the dragon and pressing with all their might against the head of

the silver creature. But nothing seemed to move. They tried again, but they were not strong enough to move the heavy metal head. "Ouch, my fingers are hurting!" Feya complained after the fifth attempt, and ran over to the little fountain with silver water to soothe her fingers. The water seemed to work wonders, for the pain disappeared immediately.

The others also refreshed themselves at the source and immediately felt better. They gathered their courage for another attempt to open the dragon. To their great astonishment, this time the head seemed to move almost by itself. The elves stood aside, for now the mist, which had previously emerged as a fine stream from the dragon's mouth, now poured thick and white from the narrow gap between the head and body.

The Voice
of the Oracle

areful!" shouted Falaroy. "The dragon is moving!" Eyela grabbed hold of the others and quick-wittedly pulled them away from the silver figure - not a moment too soon, for suddenly the dragon raised itself and stretched its heavy head up high. The gap between the head and body grew larger, broke open at other points, allowing more and more of the white mist to emerge.

The dragon raised its silver wings, almost as if it wanted to fly away. However, it stood on its hind legs and threw its head from side to side. The rigid, smooth elf silver of its body seemed to be changing. Eyela thought she could see scales on the dragon's back and legs, and the metal skin of the mysterious creature seemed to glisten.

The openings on the neck had meanwhile formed into large, gill-like organs. The dragon seemed to be gasping for air, while at the same time giving off more and more of the white mist.

"I can hardly see!" shouted Feya full of fear, reaching for the hands of her friends. The others too found the scene very eerie. "By all the elf princes of Bayala, what's happening?!" Falaroy now cried out. "The walls of the pyramid, they're moving apart!" Looking up, they really could already make out part of the sky between the white mist and the bright gleaming light.

Suddenly the room around the four companions seemed to open. The walls silently collapsed, and then the elves imagined themselves to be in a large, open field, but enveloped in a thick cloud of mist.

Sera staggered. The other elves also felt dizzy. They tried to support each other, but they felt themselves slowly losing consciousness. The last thing the friends saw was the dragon spreading its silver wings over them - then all four lost consciousness.

Feya was the first to open her eyes again. She recognised the cloudless, starry night sky, and a light wind blew through her wings and hair. But where was she? It all suddenly came back to her: the Bannwald forest, the long walk, the pyramid and also the silver dragon. With an effort, she stood up and looked around. Beside her lay Falaroy, Eyela and Sera. They too were now regaining consciousness. Behind her friends, Feya noticed a flat, stone staircase. On one side there were sharp crystals, on the other were gnarled roots. At the top of the stairs was a small space with a beautiful round stone table. Above it, a formation of metal and stone was visible. But the most impressive thing was a round surface in the middle of this formation, which continually changed its shape: one moment it was a round surface with flame-like symbols, then it seemed to dissolve in air, leaving just a mouth-like opening.

"THE ORACLE!" the thought struck Feya. Everyone in Bayala knew about the place, at least from stories. "We're at the top of Oracle Mountain! How on earth did we get here?"

The others had meanwhile recovered, and now stood beside her in amazement. They were all silent, for it was dangerous to speak in face of the Oracle. As there was a full moon, everything could be seen clearly. Falaroy was the first to discover the two ancient guardian elves Menatea and Tulon. As if frozen to stone, they stood to the left and right of the mighty Elf Oracle. Normally they guarded it only during the day, as it was too dangerous even for the ancient guardians during the night. Yet something seemed to fix them to the spot.

The gentle wind had meanwhile grown a little stronger, and the four companions thought they could hear a faint whistling or whispering. Menatea and Tulon, the two guardians, did not move. Not even their hair blew in the wind. "Spirits," whispered Sera reverentially. "They are elf spirits!" Eyela shook her head carefully. "No," she whispered. "The guardians are under the protection of the Oracle. And the Oracle governs the forces of nature. Nothing can happen to them. My father once told me that." A flash of lightning hit the ground directly in front of the elves. They had a terrible fright when the thunder rumbled menacingly above them. Then it was again almost silent, just a soft whispering could be heard:

"Sssssssss..........." Was it the wind again? No. "Sssssseeeera...." The name of Eyela's sister was clear to hear. "The Oracle is speaking to us," whispered Feya, fully of inner excitement, and the others also barely dared to breathe.

"*Sera, daughter of King Baramah,*" they now heard the Oracle saying quietly but clearly. The voice now sounded unreal and hollow, as if it were coming from the depth of the mountain.

> "*Heavy lies the mist on the land of the elves.*
> *Fate has been interwoven with the mist since that night.*
> *The sisters' bond was torn and with the mist everything*
> *sank into oblivion. Yet the night is growing darker*
> *and the day of reckoning is approaching.*
> *Hair into fire, fire into smoke.*
> *One curl is enough, and fate will obey.*"

Then the Oracle fell silent. The friends looked at each other at a loss. What was the meaning of these words? Falaroy pointed down the valley towards the gentle slopes and hills that were becoming visible at the foot of Oracle Mountain in the moonlight. Before, thick mist used to form there only during the day, but now thick clouds drifted through the valleys even at night. Falaroy looked to the others and whispered: "I think the Oracle wants to tell us that Bayala will sink in the mist if we don't do something.

The sisters' bond...It seems as if all our future is linked to the fate of Sera and her vanished twin sister." Falaroy cast a worried look at the sky, where dark clouds were forming. Eyela and Sera looked deep into each other's eyes, for they both had the same thought: Could it be that their sister Surah was in fact still alive? The Oracle had spoken of the bond having been torn, but the meaning of these words allowed many possibilities.

Sera tried to remember the exact words of the Oracle.

...Hair into fire, fire into smoke.
One curl is enough, and fate will obey...

Sera reflected a while on the meaning of these words, then she bent down and picked up a little sharp-edged stone at her feet. She took hold of her hair and cut off a curl of her beautiful elf hair with the little stone.

She took the curl and went up the steps to the Oracle to the large, round stone slab. The other elves watched her anxiously, as nobody knew how the Oracle would react. She placed the strand of hair on the slab and stepped back. Suddenly, the two elf guardians raised their staffs toward the sky.

The huge dark clouds hung above Oracle Mountain, and suddenly there was another flash of lighting. This time it struck exactly on the stone table, and Sera's lock of hair went up in a bright, blazing flame. Fine smoke rose from the spot. Above the elves' heads, this smoke seemed to gather and become denser. Eyela and the others watched in amazement as the smoke formed the shape of a small, green bird. The little bird fluttered a while above their heads, then disappeared into the night. The moment the little bird had disappeared, a great shadow covered the full moon and the elves saw that a huge dragon was approaching from above. It was evidently the same dragon they had seen in the pyramid, but it now seemed much more powerful and its skin appeared to glisten in the moonlight in all the colours of the rainbow. Reverentially, but also in fear, the elves bowed down as the huge creature approached from the sky and spread its wings over them. It grew dark.

Way to the north, in the palace of the dark elf princess Nuray, Surah awoke with a start in her bed. She was wide awake at once, for something had knocked on the window of her bed chamber. Surah listened. There it was again! It sounded like someone scratching or throwing small stones against the windowpane. Surah quickly threw on her bathrobe and ran over to the window where she supposed the noise was coming from. But outside everything seemed dark and peaceful. She could only hear the icy wind from the north blowing through the pinnacles and towers of the palace. But there was that sound again!

Surah opened the window a crack, and what she saw astounded her. On the stone windowsill, there sat a small, green bird tapping ceaselessly with its beak against the window frame. Birds were very rare here in the far north, and when they appeared it was only large birds of prey who had adapted to the harsh conditions of life in the mountains.

Surah reached out carefully in order not to scare the little visitor away, but astonishingly, the bird showed no fear whatsoever, but gracefully perched on Surah's hand. She drew her arm with the bird back inside and closed the window. Then she noticed a wonderful thing: starting at the point where the bird sat on her arm, a pleasant warmth was spreading through Surah's body. Even the skin lost its paleness, and seemed to turn a gentle pink colour. She had to smile, as she had never seen anything like it. She set the little bird down on the bedside table beside her bed, looked at it for a long time, then fell asleep.

Not only Surah felt warmth on her skin during that night. Nuray, the dark ruler, lay in her bed writhing. However, in contrast to Surah, it was not the graceful warmth of a little bird that kept her awake, but the symbols on her shoulders that had again started to burn. She tossed from side to side, tried to soothe the pain with silver water, but nothing was any use. Only in the early hours of the morning Nuray also gradually found peace.

Surah's Secret

uray slept. In her dreams she saw her mother standing alone on a rock protruding over a dark abyss. Uhara's hair blew in the icy wind and she seemed to be calling, but Nuray could not hear her. The whistling of the wind was much too loud. "Mother!" called Nuray. "Mother, I'm here! Can't you hear me?" She wanted to fly to Uhara, but something seemed to be holding her back. Nuray wanted to run to her. But her legs had already sunk into the soggy soil of the forest. Nuray desperately tried to free herself, reached out for plants that grew fast toward her and twisted her body in all directions, but she just sank deeper and deeper.

Nuray screamed... and awoke from her nightmare. She lay on the bed, breathing heavily. A window had opened during the storm in the night, and icy cold now penetrated the room. The dark princess raised herself from her bed with difficulty, for the burning symbols on her shoulders were still very painful. She ran over to the open window and closed it. In doing so, her gaze was drawn to the opposite side of the palace, and she noticed a fine green light in one of the many windows. "That's Surah's chamber," thought Nuray, and a curious uneasiness overcame her. "I wonder if she's already awake. That green glow is strange." She tried to see exactly what it might be, but the wind was blowing thick fog down from the mountains, obstructing all her efforts.

Nuray thought a while about what she had seen. Since Surah had disappeared so mysteriously that night at Shadow Rock, she had regarded her foster sister with great suspicion. She could not explain how Surah was already back in the palace the day after her disappearance. Of course, she didn't let anyone notice her doubts or ask any questions, but the princess of darkness wanted to get to the bottom of the secret at all events. Turag, her army commander, had promised his help after Nuray had apologised to him for her anger the day after the events at Shadow Rock.

The dark ruler put on a warm robe and ran across to the door of her chamber that opened toward the main corridor of the south wing. On tiptoes, so that nobody would notice her, she hurried along the corridors. The palace was huge. It took her a long time to get from one wing of the building to the other.

"Hopefully Surah won't wake up in the meantime," thought Nuray anxiously and ran faster.

Soon she was standing in front of the room that her foster sister had arranged after Uhara's death.

Nuray bent down and carefully peeped through the keyhole.

She saw Surah on her bed, still peacefully sleeping. Her cover, made of elf silk, had slipped to the floor. As the dark princess had already observed from the window of her chamber, a fine green light filled the room. Nuray's eyes gradually got used to the weak light and she could now see where the mysterious green light was coming from. At the top right-hand corner of a wardrobe decorated with beautiful carvings there was a little bird. It was not moving, but just sat there as if it wanted to guard Surah's sleep. Its eyes were the colour of emerald and glowed as if filled with inner fire. Nuray felt the pain on her skin again becoming stronger. "I've never seen such a bird here in the Shadow Kingdom. I wonder how it got here?" Nuray spied a while longer through the keyhole into Surah's room, but as her pain was increasing, she decided to go back to her chamber. Suddenly her gaze fell upon a wooden chest with iron fittings in the furthest corner of the room. It was open, and Nuray saw small dragon figures glistening in all the colours of the rainbow inside. Her heart started pounding! They could only be figures from the vaulted hall where she herself and Ophira had been just a little while ago. "Surah has been in the ancestral halls and has stolen those figures," thought Nuray angrily. But why hadn't she therefore had a curse put on her by the spirits of the deceased ancestors? After all, it was forbidden to change even the slightest detail in the vaulted halls. The dark elf princess had a sudden thought. "Of course, royal blood flows through Surah's veins! She's one of Baramah's daughters. That's what protects her from the curse." She felt envy and resentment seize her heart, and the desire to fulfil her mother's legacy grew inside her. But she had to control herself. The observations she had just made might be very useful.

The dark princess carefully crept away. She started to run faster, but when she turned the next corner, she had a terrible fright, for she almost ran into Ophira.

"Aunt!" she hissed in a suppressed voice. "Why did you frighten me? And what are you doing at this place so early in the morning?" Nuray's heart beat faster. "I'm sorry," replied Ophira calmly. "But I wanted to ask you the same thing."

Nuray also slowly recovered from the fright, and she looked silently into her aunt's eyes for a while. Ophira was very close to Nuray - but could she really trust her? After all, she had led Nuray down into the deep, dangerous vaulted halls without warning her what dangers awaited her down there. And yet it was her aunt who had saved her when she lost consciousness. Nuray was uncertain.

"Strange things are happening in Surah's room," she finally said very slowly. Ophira raised her eyebrows. "You've been looking through the keyhole!" she said, and an almost imperceptible smile flit across her face. The idea that the princess of darkness Nuray had stood before a closed door like a thief looking through the keyhole filled Ophira with a certain satisfaction. "Surah doesn't possess much. What is there to see in her room?" she said calmly, for she did not want to show in any way how curious she was. Nuray looked at her aunt penetratingly and replied: "This is not the right place to talk about it. We can meet in my chamber at midday and I will tell you what I saw. I will also send a message to Turag asking him to attend."

This thought made Ophira uneasy, for in her eyes Turag was not to be trusted. But she didn't reveal her thoughts. "Very well, as you wish," she remarked casually. "I will be there."

Turag was the first to knock at Nuray's door at midday. The dark princess opened the door and the army commander stepped in. "You called for me?" he asked with a slight bow. Nuray nodded without a word and offered him a place at her precious table, manufactured from fine elf silver. Shortly after, Ophira was at the door. "I'm glad to see you both," said Nuray, smiling a little. "Can I serve you something to eat?" she asked, but Turag and Ophira declined with thanks.

Nuray took a seat at the table with the others and started to report what she had seen that morning in Surah's room. "Dragons... Surah has stolen dragon figures from the vaulted halls," declared Ophira, her voice trembling with excitement when Nuray finished her report. "This worries me very much, for these figures supposedly have great magic powers." Turag and Nuray looked at each other knowingly, and the princess of darkness nodded almost imperceptibly. This meant that Turag should let Ophira in on the events that the two had observed when Surah disappeared at Shadow Rock.

When Ophira heard about that, she finally lost all control and shouted furiously: "Surah, that little elf beast! I'm sure she knows something! We mustn't allow her to endanger your mother's legacy. The time has come to put Uhara's plan into action and subjugate the entire elf kingdom. You, Nuray, shall be the ruler of all Bayala. And I will stand at your side!"

Turag looked at Ophira uncomprehendingly. "What power does Surah have that she can harm us?" he asked, looking from Ophira to Nuray. "What does she suspect and how can she endanger the legacy of the great Uhara?" Only now did Ophira notice that, in her excitement, she had said things that only she and Nuray should know. She clenched her fists and the dark princess looked at her reproachfully. Now there was no choice but to let Turag into the secrets about

Surah. Nuray looked to the ground, remained silent for a while, and then started speaking again. She spoke of Uhara's journey to Oracle Mountain a long time ago, and the words she heard there. She told the story of Surah's kidnapping and the end of King Baramah. The dark ruler also spoke of how her mother despaired because her striving for power was not fulfilled, and of her tragic death.

Turag listened calmly to the whole story, without interrupting Nuray once. When Nuray had finished, he stood up, folded his arms and, after a while, said: "Your mother's fate explains why the shadows in our kingdom are becoming ever darker, and the fog is swallowing up the north of Bayala more and more. Uhara selfishly interpreted the Oracle to her own advantage, and the Oracle has taken bitter revenge. Unfortunately there is no way back. We must continue on the path we have taken and ensure that a decision is made. We Shadow Elves are to rule over Bayala! Let us lose no more time, for who knows what will happen otherwise." However, Turag silently thought: "If only you knew that I've been aware of this story for a long time. I will be the one to rule this land one day."

Ophira too had meanwhile recovered her composure. "Then let us make a plan," she suggested. "We must already make decisions today, but nobody apart from us three must ever find out, otherwise we are lost." "You're right, aunt," Nuray agreed. "We must act soon, for this very evening Surah may use her dragon magic to bring harm upon us." "The dragons!" Turag suddenly exclaimed. "They could be the answer to all our questions. We'll go into Surah's room and take one of her figures from the wooden chest. We saw at Shadow Rock what she does with the dragons, we could do the same thing."

Ophira looked at Turag in fear and replied: "You know that can be very dangerous. None of us knows the true power of the dragons. This attempt could possibly cost us our lives!" Nuray looked at her aunt resolutely. "Then we should never have gone into the vaulted halls," she said brusquely. "There we exposed ourselves to the greatest dangers, and I almost died of pain." She glanced at Turag. "You're right. We'll take one of Surah's silver figures and discover the secret of the dragons." "As you both wish," Ophira remarked in a cool manner. "You, Nuray, are the princess in this kingdom and can decide what must be done. If we want to be sure that Surah doesn't notice anything, we should go to her chamber in the afternoon. At that time she's always in the old library in the north wing. We can then choose one or several dragons from the wooden chest in her room and take them away." "Then let us do it," Turag confirmed resolutely. "Maybe we'll also get to the bottom of the secret of the little bird. We'll meet back here this afternoon."

Light and Shadow

phira was right. In the early afternoon, Surah always went to the old library. The mysterious old scripts and books from past times fascinated her and she secretly hoped to find answers to her questions there. Since the bird had been with her, it had not left her side. Even when she left her chamber. She hid it under her cloak and it snuggled up against her skin.

Nuray, Ophira and Turag watched Surah leave her room, and shortly after the three were standing before the chest with the magic figures. The dark princess had a key to all the chambers in the palace, so it was easy for her to gain access. "Look how artistically crafted the dragons are!" exclaimed Nuray. The silver figures shimmered delicately in all the colours of the rainbow and their features were in such fine detail that they almost seemed to be alive.

"Let's take one quickly and get out of here," said Turag hastily, looking around uncertainly. "Who knows when Surah will be back from the library." "Normally she's away for quite a while," replied Ophira calmly. "But you're right, we shouldn't hang around here too long." "Let's take one of the figures from the bottom, then it won't be so obvious," Nuray suggested. She reached into the chest. A sharp pain shot through her arm. She bit her lip so that the others would not notice. She quickly withdrew her arm from the chest, holding a little figure in her hand. "We'll take this one," she said, promptly placing it in a little bag made of course linen. "Come on, let's get out of here fast." Nuray straightened everything out, then the three crept out of the room and back to their chambers.

When it was slowly getting dark in the late afternoon, Nuray, Turag and Ophira met at Shadow Rock. The fog hung thickly around the stone pinnacles, and the icy wind blew down from the north. The three Shadow Elves flew up to the highest gallery of the building, which they had selected as their place of action. Nuray was carrying the little bag with the dragon figure from Surah's room. She cautiously took the figure out and placed it carefully on the floor. All three remained silent, for they each realised the potential danger they could face.

"Are you ready?" asked Nuray softly. Turag and Ophira nodded. The princess of darkness bent down and started to unscrew the head of the little dragon figure. It was attached to the silver body with such a fine thread that the joint between head and body was barely visible. Nuray carefully continued unscrewing. Turag tried to remain calm, but he continually rubbed his large hands together, and Ophira kept looking around nervously. Finally the head came off the figure, and fine white mist poured out from inside the dragon's body. The mist quickly became thicker. It started to envelop the three elves and to wrap itself around them like a fine cloth.

Nuray noticed how she alternately felt hot and cold. She glanced at her hands, which appeared to be dissolving in the mist. At her side, Turag and Ophira also now hardly seemed recognisable. A strange sensation overcame the dark princess. She felt as light as a feather, but everything seemed to hurt as if a great fever had caught hold of her. She was no longer in control of her senses. Her eyes, ears, skin and mind seemed to be melting, forming a whole. She felt herself turning to mist and light. The heavy clouds and the storm dispersed, and suddenly the sun shone brightly in the sky. Nuray was pulled up by a powerful maelstrom. She felt herself becoming one with the sun and the light, and time seemed to stand still.

Then suddenly everything went dark. The feeling of heaviness returned. Nuray's pulse started to beat fast, and she sensed that her body was regaining its shape, which it had just lost to the mist. Soon she was able to see her arms and legs. She looked to her side. Beside her she saw the shadows of Ophira and Turag. Their eyes slowly became accustomed to the surroundings and the princess of the north now realised that it was not really dark. The sun was shining brightly in the sky, and because Nuray had herself merged with the glaring light of the sun, any weaker light first seemed to be just a shadow.

A little later, the three elves had recovered their original forms. They looked around in awe, for they realised that they were just above Oracle Mountain. They simply hovered and barely needed to move their wings, for a gentle breeze kept them floating in the air.

"How did we get here?" asked Nuray when she was able to speak. She only had to look into Ophira's and Turag's eyes to know that they had also made the same mysterious journey. "I don't know," whispered Ophira uneasily. "It must be the magic of the dragon figures. So that's what Surah does every evening." She looked around anxiously and then whispered: "Careful, it's dangerous to speak on Oracle Mountain!" "I think we're safe here up in the air," Turag tried to reassure her. "But you're right, we shouldn't provoke the anger of Oracle Mountain."

"Look, on the ground!" whispered Nuray astonished. "Those are footprints. It appears that someone has been up on Oracle Mountain just recently." "Sun Elves!" hissed Ophira, unable to conceal her excitement. "The footprints are small and fine. It can only have been Sun Elves. What did they want up here?" "I fear they are on the track of the secret of the two princesses, Surah and Sera," said Turag. "We can only hope that the Oracle didn't tell them too much." "Shall we ask the Oracle ourselves?" suggested Nuray, but Ophira dismissed the idea. "That's much too dangerous," she cautioned. "Just think what happened to your mother." Turag agreed, then continued: "There's no more time to lose. When we get back to the palace we should devise a plan fast. The days of decision are approaching." Nuray nodded seriously. "But how will we get away from here?" she wondered. Meanwhile the sun was relentlessly burning their white skin. Ophira and Turag were also suffering, for the Shadow Elves were not used to being exposed to sunlight. "Surah was never away for long," Nuray remarked. "So there must be a fast way back. But if we fly during the day and walk at night, the journey will take several days, and there will be great concern in the palace at our disappearance."

"Above all, we must get out of the sun and into the shade," groaned Ophira. "My skin is already burning like fire. Let's fly a little toward the north. Where the Shadow Kingdom starts, it's cooler and darker, and we can discuss what to do."

The three elves quickly distanced themselves from Oracle Mountain, and soon the sun disappeared behind thick clouds.

Shortly after, they were sitting on the bank of a river on the gnarled trunk of a tree that had fallen in the storm. Nuray was cooling her burnt skin with the clear water. An unpleasant thought overcame her. Soon it would be dark, and in this area there was far and wide nowhere for them to sleep. The idea of sleeping outside was extremely unsettling, but she avoided showing her unease. She casually asked: "Well, you two, have you any idea how we can get away from here?" Turag and Ophira looked at each other questioningly, but they had no more idea than the dark princess herself. "If we only knew what magic Surah had used," said Ophira morosely. Turag was chewing on a piece of moor weed root. He was terribly hungry, and it was the only edible thing he could find. "Surah's magic would probably not help us either," he reflected. "Who knows, maybe each little dragon has its own magic that works differently for all who use it."

Nuray was cold and she put her hands in the pockets of her long red cloak to warm them. To her astonishment, she felt the little dragon's head that was still there. She took it out and looked at it carefully. On its cheeks there were fine wavelines similar to water, and the forehead was decorated with a sun ornament. Ophira and Turag also looked at the engravings with interest. "Sun and water...," remarked Ophira. "That must definitely mean something. After all, the sun brought us here. Maybe the water is the key to our return." "But how?" asked Nuray. "We can't just throw the head into the river." "No, we shouldn't do that," agreed Turag. "But we could sprinkle some water on the head to see what happens. Let's try."

Nuray placed the little dragon's head on some soft moss. She collected a little water in a plant chalice and carefully allowed some to drip onto the silver face. First nothing happened, so Nuray sprinkled a little more water onto the head. A fine trickle found its way through the moss to the riverbank. When the first drops that had been in contact with the dragon fell into the river, something strange happened: the water started flowing faster. Small waves formed, quickly turning into large, foaming masses of water. The river became a wild current, overflowing the banks and tearing away the first trees. Nuray, Turag and Ophira quickly saw the danger and tried to flee. "Quick, get away!" shouted Turag, but he was too late. With a roar, the water crashed down over the three elves and swept them away. Nuray thought their end had come. But strangely, she soon realised that she had not drowned. Much rather, she felt like part of the current, as if she had herself turned to water. Despite the roaring maelstrom around her, her breathing was calm and even.

Nuray felt like a young child again, travelling with her mother on the great, black river far in the north. There too, the water had been wild, but the sense of security in her mother's company had banished any fear, and she had fallen asleep in Uhara's arms. And now, her eyes were also feeling heavy. The water swirled, but Nuray could feel herself falling asleep. She gave in to her feelings, and she soon lost consciousness.

When Nuray awoke, she was lying on the bank of a small mountain stream that flowed through the rocks at the foot of her huge palace. Beside her lay Turag and Ophira. Both seemed dry and unharmed. When the princess of darkness sat up, Turag and Ophira also came to. "Let's go back to the palace fast," suggested Turag. "I've had enough adventure for today." "We can be glad to still be alive," agreed Nuray. "Who knows, maybe our disappearance has caused a commotion." "I don't think so, Nuray," Ophira now remarked. "It's not even dark, as if time has stood still since we met at Shadow Rock." "That's true!" shouted Nuray in amazement. "But how can it be possible?" "Don't forget that the dragon figures are from the vaults," Ophira observed. "In the ancestral halls, time has no power over what happens there.

It may be the same for the figures and their magic. But let's now fly back to the palace. It's starting to get dark and I'm cold." The three elves stood up and, in the last daylight, flew back to the palace.

The Face in the Mirror

he next morning, far away from all these events in the land of the Sun Elves, the sun was rising. Eyela rose from her bed, combed her hair and put on a morning robe. She could still not believe what had happened at Oracle Mountain, and how she and her friends had come back to the kingdom of the Sun Elves.

Eyela sat down at her table and started thinking. She tried to recollect the adventure that she had experienced together with Feya, Falaroy and Sera...

That night, when the Oracle had spoken to her and the great dragon had descended on them, it had grown dark around her and her friends. Eyela still thought she could feel the dragon's great claws grabbing her and pulling her up into the air. But what happened then she did not know. Only on the following morning was Eyela able to remember.

She and her friends had woken up in a meadow, not far from Summergreen House, as the first rays of sun shone through the high treetops.

Since that morning in the meadow, two days had now passed and none of the four elves could explain how they had got back from Oracle Mountain.

Eyela rose from her table and walked up and down nervously. She felt a great unease inside, which did not abate all morning. She tried to distract herself with little jobs, but her thoughts kept wandering.

Then, at lunchtime, she flew to Summergreen House, for she had arranged to meet Feya, Falaroy and Sera there. Together they wanted to devise a plan.

From a distance she could already hear Feya and Falaroy laughing. They were riding their horses on the large meadow in front of the house, chasing each other and having fun. They both seemed very boisterous. "You call that riding?" shouted Feya provocatively with a challenging grin. "Even our little elf children can ride better than that." Falaroy bent down low over his horse and whispered something in its ear. "Just wait, I'll show you, you cheeky elf!" he called out to Feya with a laugh. "The first one to get to the giant old oak tree over there is the winner." And in a dash he was already off. Eyela too had to laugh, but secretly she felt a little jealous. After all, it wasn't so long ago, on the night of the Bannwald Festival, that Falaroy had been making eyes at her. When Falaroy and Feya returned from their chase, they were joking and arguing about who had won the race. They then saw Eyela and dismounted from their horses. "Hello, beautiful princess," Falaroy greeted Eyela laughing. Eyela felt a slight stab in her heart when she looked into the elf's bright, young eyes. "No, he truly doesn't think about the effect of his impetuous charm in our hearts," thought Eyela. But she quickly turned the conversation to the actual subject of their meeting. "Where is Sera?" she asked, looking around. "We wanted to discuss and reflect on the mysterious events of recent days."

"I don't know," replied Feya, and Falaroy also shrugged his shoulders. "She should have arrived by now." "Come on, let us fly to her leaf-house," suggested Eyela. "It's not far, and I've a feeling something's not right." "That's a good idea, let's fly, because you can't ride," Falaroy remarked, grinning cheekily at Feya. "Just wait!" called Feya. "You'll soon see how well I can fly!" Eyela just shook her head. Actually, she too was up for some fun, but the events of the past days weighed on her soul like a shadow. She flew off before Feya and Falaroy, who followed her laughing and joking.

Sera's leaf-house was high in the branches of a giant tree. When they first got there, they thought the entrance was locked. But when Eyela touched the handle of the door, which was woven from fine lianas, she noticed that it was open. "How strange, there's no sound," whispered Feya. "Can we just walk in?" Eyela carefully opened the door and the three elves peered inside the room.

Feya and Eyela knew of Sera's fondness of all things green, but they were amazed at the attention to detail with which the room had been furnished. Everything seemed to be made of plants, leaves and flowers. How Sera managed to preserve the blossom and the green for all time and to retain the bright colours was her own special secret and an art that only very few elves understood.

But they then discovered something else that made them very uneasy: at the far end of the room there was a mirror. This mirror was so big that you could see yourself from head to toe in it. Before it stood Sera, perfectly still as if she had turned into a pillar of salt. But what was even more remarkable: the image reflected in the mirror seemed to be burning and red flames licked at the reflected figure. Falaroy immediately wanted to run to Sera's aid, but Eyela held him back. "Careful, Falaroy," she whispered. "This mirror is special. It is very old. My father gave it to us just before he died. It often seems to have a will of its own and never gives an accurate reflection. Come on, we'll go over to Sera carefully." Feya and Falaroy followed her in silence.

When the three elves were standing directly behind Sera, they noticed something strange. Not only that the mirror distorted the image with flames, no, it seemed also not to reflect Sera as she really was. The stature, arms and hands seemed to resemble those of the princess, but her facial features were significantly harder. The robe the elf in the mirror was wearing was completely different from Sera's light morning robe, as it was blacker and heavier.

The flames licked menacingly at the dark elf, but she didn't seem to notice the danger, but just stood there rigidly like Sera herself. Eyela, Feya and Falaroy noticed one thing only now: a little green bird was sitting on the bent left arm of the reflected figure, partially concealed by the dark robe. It gracefully snuggled its little head against the elf's hip without even the slightest fear. You almost had the impression that the bird had a special magic power against the fire and emitted a protective force.

Sera stood there as if spellbound. Her eyes and those of her mirror reflection seemed to captivate each other. Looking very closely, it appeared that fine flames were flaring up from the eyes in the mirror and being absorbed by Sera's gaze.

Suddenly the flames grew stronger and swallowed up the elf in the mirror. Soon only her silhouette was just dimly recognisable. Sera's whole body started trembling and she clenched her fists. Soon only a red sea of flames was visible in the mirror. Sera's body twitched as if she were in great pain. Eyela could no longer bear it, but just as she wanted to intervene Sera cried out and the image in the mirror faded. The flames disappeared and all that remained was the image of Sera, who was standing before the mirror exhausted and breathing heavily.

A while later, the four elves were sitting discussing together in Summergreen House. Sera had fortunately recovered quickly from her shock and was unharmed.

"Sera, was it you we saw in the mirror?" asked Feya. Eyela's younger sister looked at the ground helplessly. "I don't know," she replied. "First it seemed to be me, but then it didn't." She continued: "The elf looked very similar to me, yet it was also completely different. What do you think, dear sister?" Sera looked at Eyela questioningly. Eyela reflected a while and then slowly replied: "I think it must have been Surah we saw."

The words came from her mouth almost torturously. Her face was serious, for she realised the significance of what she was saying. "Maybe she's alive and in great danger!" She continued: "But even if it really was Surah in the mirror, it doesn't help us. We don't know whether she's alive or where she is. Father also appeared before me a few days ago at the pond, even though he's dead." "You're right, sister," Sera confirmed Eyela's words. "I had a similar thought. But we shouldn't get carried away with suppositions. Surah is part of me, and even if there's just the slightest hope of finding her, then I'm prepared to risk everything - even my own life."

Eyela nodded, while Feya and Falaroy looked at the ground in consternation. Feya was visibly struggling with her feelings. Falaroy, on the other hand, just seemed to be sad. Since he had come to the elf girls a few days before, he had become very fond of them and the thought that one of them might be in danger filled him with disquiet. They all remained silent for a while, then Eyela plucked up courage and said: "Surah is our sister and, like us, a daughter of King Baramah. Sera, we will set off to look for her, even if it takes an eternity or costs us our lives. You, dear Feya, stay here with Falaroy to stand by our people. Who knows what dangers await us and all the Sun Elves. Sera, let us pack our things and set off first thing in the morning. We mustn't lose any more time."

Falaroy jumped up. "No way will you two go alone!" he called out in excitement. "Eyela, you are Baramah's eldest daughter and, after his death, the heir to his throne. For me you are the queen of our kingdom and I will follow you wherever you go." Sera and Eyela looked at him in surprise. "I too will come...," whispered Feya softly, as if she could herself hardly believe what she was saying. "I too will come!" she then cried out loud. Eyela looked at her in amazement. Then she said: "Dear friends, I am very grateful for your wanting to accompany us, but are you aware of the dangers that we may encounter? The adventure in the Bannwald forest was perhaps just a harmless foretaste of what's to come. I think it would be better for you to stay here and not put yourselves in such danger."

"There's no question of it!" shouted Falaroy defiantly. "There are enough strong elves who can look after things here. It will take special powers to stop me from following you."

"And nothing will prevent me either from joining you in the search for Surah," said Feya, her voice still trembling slightly. "What should I do around here if my best friends are all away? I wouldn't be able to sleep at night. The risks facing us seem a more pleasant alternative!"

Eyela hesitated a while. She was clearly struggling with herself inside. On the one hand, she did not want to put her friends in danger, but, on the other hand, Falaroy and Feya might be of great help.

"Well," she finally said. "if you all absolutely want to, you can accompany Sera and me on our journey to the unknown. I will be glad to have you at our side. But you must be aware that it may also be our last journey." "I will go with you wherever you wish," said Falaroy resolutely. Tears came to

Feya's eyes. "I don't know if I can really be of any help," she said softly. "But you can rely on me being always at your side."

The Book of Elves

On the morning of the same day, Surah had gone to the palace library to look for a book on the birds of Bayala. She wanted at all costs to find out about her green feathered friend, for she could not understand how the little creature had been able to survive the harsh climate of the north and get to her.

The library was a large, plain room with only one window, whose walls held mighty shelves with countless books. Surah had never tried to take a book from the top shelves, as they reached almost up to the ceiling of the high room. However, that morning she had noticed a book that aroused her curiosity. It was on one of the top shelves, was exceptionally thick, and on its shabby binding the elf noticed a little mirror. The little light in the room had reflected in it, dazzling Surah for a moment. But to get to the book one problem had to be overcome: it was really difficult to fly in the library, as there was hardly any light. Surah waited a while until some dark clouds had drifted past the window, allowing a little more light into the room. Although it was now somewhat brighter, it was a great effort for Surah to fly up to the ceiling to the book. Only on her third attempt was she able to grasp the book. She immediately returned to the ground and carefully wiped off the dust. She looked at the book closely. On the cover, she read in large letters and a very old script: *The Book of Elves*

The little mirror that had dazzled her was on the spine of the volume, but when Surah looked into it she got a fright. In the mirror, the elf could see only darkness, occasionally interrupted by a few red flames burning from the edges. Otherwise nothing. The elf looked around anxiously, but there was nobody else in the library beside herself. She put the book under her morning robe and quickly returned to her chamber. There she sat on the bed and started leafing through the pages. The little green bird seemed to sense Surah's disquiet, flew to her and settled on her shoulder, nestling gracefully and gently against her left cheek.

Surah tried to comprehend what she saw in the book. She was unable to decipher many of the old, hand-written texts, for the letters must have been from a time long past. However, the individual pages were decorated with wonderfully drawn pictures, so Surah was mostly able to guess the meaning.

The book told the story of a flourishing time gone by, when the elf people of Bayala were governed by a mighty ruler. At that time, the land was not yet divided into two halves by the impenetrable fog below Oracle Mountain. The elves celebrated great festivals in honour of the sun, the earth, fire, water and wind. Everyone seemed to be happy. There were always dragons at the side of the mighty ruler, using their fire to provide valuable assistance in building up the land.

Surah immersed herself in the pictures. She noticed that every seventh drawing showed the head of a dragon. To judge the character of the dragons by the pictures, they appeared to have been proud and brave, but also shy in a secretive manner. On the pages below the drawings there were curious symbols that Surah was not able to decipher. She assumed they were the names of the noble creatures or perhaps even magic formulas that formed an entity with the fiery magic of the dragon pictures.

Lost in thought, Surah looked at the pictures, for she felt she had already seen these dragons somewhere before. Then she remembered the dark mirror on the book binding. She again looked into it, hoping perhaps to recognise something.

First it seemed that nothing had changed. The red flames were still licking at the edges, but now they were not quite as strong. Otherwise she saw only the darkness that had made her feel so uneasy the first time she had looked in the mirror. But this time Surah could not take her eyes away. She had a feeling of falling into the darkness surrounded by flames. The flames licked at her from the side. She feared she would now burn and screamed, but to her great astonishment the fire was not hot. On the contrary, a mysterious, penetrating coldness seemed to emanate from the flames.

The fire crept up Surah's arms and legs, and started to burn her clothes and even her hair. She could feel the warmth of her little bird, nestling against her, but the cold of the flames seemed to be stronger. Surah tried to extinguish the fire with her hands, writhing to and fro... and finally tore her gaze away from the mirror that had taken possession of her. Shivering with cold, she sat on her bed breathing heavily. She quickly threw a bed sheet over the book so as not to be tempted to look in the mirror again. She took a cloth from a little cupboard and hastily wrapped the ancient volume in it. Then she carefully placed it in the chest in which she kept the dragon figures.

All of a sudden, Surah realised where she had seen the dragon faces in the book before. They very much resembled the figures she had discovered during her excursions to the vaulted halls. Surah froze at the thought of the danger she may have been in when she had taken some of the figures up to her room. To all appearances, the room with the secret figures was a very special place. "How old might the silver dragon and elf figures kept in the vaulted hall be, and what story might they tell?" Surah wondered. She shuddered at the thought that she had, without any foreboding, gone into the magic mist from inside the figures. She quickly closed the chest, changed her clothes and left the room.

The whole of the following day, Surah's thoughts were absorbed by what she had discovered in the book. A strong inner feeling of unease gripped her. She sensed that events were approaching that would change her life forever. As much as this worried and frightened her, she still yearned for the day on which she would find answers to all the questions that were burning her soul.

Every day at noon all the Shadow Elves who lived in the palace met in the dining room and a large banquet was prepared with noble dishes. Nuray and her following met there for lunch. Everyone who wanted could come, even the servants of the dark ruler. Uhara had introduced this custom while she was still alive, of course not without selfish reasons, for she thus ensured that all the servants in the palace obeyed her practically without question. Nuray had realised this when she was still a child, and continued the custom after her mother's death.

Surah always sat apart from the other elves while eating, and spoke to them only very rarely. On this day she was particularly quiet and introverted. Ophira, who had come just after Surah, watched her very closely. Nuray too, who was standing right beside her aunt, seemed to notice something. "Just look, Princess," Ophira said quietly. "Surah seems worried. She's just pretending to eat and looks really nervous." "You're right, Ophira," replied Nuray. "Something seems to be preoccupying her. But be careful! She mustn't notice that we are observing her." "Let's keep watching her discreetly," said Ophira. "And tonight, before she goes to bed, we'll meet Turag outside her bed chamber to find out what's worrying her."

Just a little later, Surah left the dining room and went back to her room. Nuray and Ophira watched her suspiciously.

In the evening the blood-red sun set behind the great mountains in Nuray's Shadow Kingdom. For the first time in a long while it had again come out for a few hours in the north of Bayala. Pale and almost shamefaced, its countenance could be made out behind the dark afternoon clouds. When the last rays disappeared over the horizon, the sky seemed to be aflame, and it took a while for the clouds to change from glowing red to dark violet and, finally, the usual blackness of the night.

Surah stood at the window of her chamber watching nature's dramatic display. Her friend, the little green bird, sat on her left shoulder, rubbing its soft feathers gently against her ear. Surah was holding the book with the mirror. The whole afternoon, she had been walking up and down in her room pondering what she could do. For a brief moment she had toyed with the idea of going to Shadow Rock with one of the dragon figures to turn herself into mist. But since Surah had studied the Book of Elves, she felt uneasy at the thought. The power of the ancient dragons seemed too daunting. And yet, something had to happen! Of that Surah was certain.

She gently stroked the soft feathers of her feathered friend and could feel great warmth flowing from the little animal. "My friend," she whispered. "If only you could help me. If only I knew why my heart feels so empty." The little bird flew up, flapping its wings eagerly. It flew around the room several times, repeatedly aiming straight for the window. It then pecked at the glass, continually repeating the procedure. Surah watched in amazement. Since the little bird had come to her, it had always behaved very calmly, just flying occasionally around the room and otherwise mostly sitting on her shoulder, the cupboard, or at night beside her bed.

"Do you want to fly outside?" she asked. "Or maybe you even want to leave me?" Surah opened the window and the icy cold from the north penetrated into the room. However, the little bird made no effort to fly away. It just kept flying outside briefly, beat its wings and flew back into the room to Surah. "What are you trying to tell me?" the elf asked thoughtfully, quickly closing the window again. "First you fly outside, only to come back in straight away, as if you wanted to take me away with you." At these words, the bird suddenly settled calmly on Surah's shoulder, nestling its delicate head against her neck. "So that's it!" Surah shouted in astonishment. "You want me to fly with you." She looked out of the window. In the darkness of the night, the outline of the mighty mountains looming up in the north could just be dimly made out. Surah knew how cold it was outside there, and that she would not survive three days in this raw wilderness. On the other hand, she could no longer stand life here in the palace, and her yearning to get to the bottom of her secret grew day by day. "What have I to lose?" she thought. "If I am to die out there, then so be it. Anything would be better than to stay in the palace and perish in uncertainty." She carefully lifted her little friend from her shoulder, placed it on her right hand and looked at it for a long while in silence. Then she said: "I am placing my fate in your little wings. Show me the way to freedom and help me solve all the puzzles that threaten to stifle my heart. We will set off first thing tomorrow morning at daybreak. I'll just pack a few things, then I'll be ready."

A smile flitted across her face. "How odd," she thought. "I'm probably going to my ruin, yet I feel lighter than ever before. If these days are to be my last, then I want them at least to be my happiest."

What Surah did not know was that Nuray, Ophira and Turag had been watching her. Just as when the three had taken the dragon figure from the chest, this time too they listened at the door to Surah's chamber and peered through the keyhole.

Ophira could hardly control herself. "She wants to flee the palace!" she hissed to Nuray. "We must stop her before she brings disaster upon us!" "No," replied Nuray. "Let her fly.

Normally it's not possible to survive out there alone. Even her little companion won't be able to help her. She may be less dangerous than here in the palace, where her snooping and transformations could cause more trouble. However, we mustn't lose any more time! We'll let Surah fly to her ruin. We are ourselves powerful enough to make a decision. I'll drum our most faithful followers together, and we'll set off first thing tomorrow. I can feel that the day my mother's legacy is to be fulfilled is not far off!

On Twisting Paths

ar away from Nuray's Palace, roughly a day's journey west of Oracle Mountain, there was a place known as *Dragon Cliff*, revered highly by all the elves of Bayala. It was a small mountain, whose jagged and rocky peak climbed skywards, making it almost impossible to reach by foot. Particularly special was the mountain peak itself because it resembled a large dragon's nest made of stone. Similar to a crater, from the edge of this nest one could peer into the centre of the mountain and look down onto several caves opening up from below. However, the passageways were too dark to be able to see anything and no elf would ever think of trying to discover the secret of these caves.

According to legend, the last great dragon had lived in the stone nest which had once been involved in the pact with the dark elf princes. Just like the entire land at the foot of Oracle Mountain, Dragon Cliff was also almost completely wrapped in a thick fog and for a long time no-one had dared to go near it. Thus, nobody had noticed the peculiar noises that had been coming from inside the crater for some time.

The next morning Surah got up very early to pack her things. She was determined to put her plan into action and to leave the palace as quickly as possible. Surah tried to be as quiet as possible because under no circumstances did she want anyone in the palace to notice her disappearance. She quickly packed something warm to wear, as well as her most important possessions. The Book of Elves was also placed between the items of clothing in her bag. Then she quickly looked around the room once more and opened the window. "Show me the way, my little friend," she whispered to the bird. "Alone, I am lost in the outside world." Surah's feathered companion spread out its small wings, fluttered away and the elf followed him.

The dark ruler had already given a few of her followers an order the evening before to prepare everything for a long journey and to pack enough supplies. She gave Turag the order to round up some of the strongest elves, then said to

Ophira: "O revered Aunt, the day has come for us to set off to take control of the entire kingdom. I feel the signs burning on my shoulders, but it is not the same fire as the last few days but rather the flames of fruition. Yet to ensure that fortune is good to us, a special magic is required," she continued. "Therefore, fly quickly to Bilara. She shall accompany us on the journey and with her elf magic turn the tide in our favour." "As you wish," replied Ophira, yet whoever looked closer would have noticed a slight twitch in her eyebrows at the mention of the name.

The elf sorceress Bilara had lived for a long time in an extinct volcano not very far from the palace. She was shy and spoke very little. Yet whoever looked into her eyes could see a magic fire blazing, a fire that burned within her. Nobody knew where she came from or how old she was because time appeared to leave no traces on her. Every now and then Nuray asked her advice about something important, apart from that, however, their paths seldom crossed, despite the short distance from the volcano to the palace. Nevertheless, Nuray was certain that she had a loyal servant in Bilara because her mother Uhara already appreciated the advice of the sorceress.

It was not only in the kingdom of the Shadow Elves that preparations were being made for a long journey. Eyela and her friends too had already saddled up the horses and made all the preparations for the imminent search for Surah. "Are you ready?" called Eyela, looking earnestly at her three companions. All the elves in the area had gathered in front of Summergreen House to bid farewell to the four friends. "As far as I'm concerned we can get going now," replied Falaroy brusquely. "The horses are ready to go and our bags are packed." "I think it's great that we're not flying or on foot but taking the horses instead," said Sera. "We can also travel at night and who knows how these dear animals can be of further use to us." Feya softly stroked the neck of her white mare and whispered a few coaxing words in its ear. She loved her horse above everything else and could not imagine being away from it for longer than a day.

Eyela turned to the numerous elves who had gathered, and said in a loud voice: "Dear friends, my sister Sera, Falaroy, Feya and I have a dangerous journey ahead of us. There are signs that the missing daughter of King Baramah, our sister Surah, is still alive. If this is true, there could well be changes in store for us soon. It is our mission to uncover this mystery, a mystery which cost my father his life and has destroyed our kingdom." An uneasiness spread among the elves because nobody knew about the events of the last few days. The King's daughter had tears in her eyes. "Do not worry about us. We will return again to you fit and healthy. Please stay here at home and look after everything here. We will ride north, to the place from where the impenetrable fog spreads out further and further over the entire land. There we hope to solve the riddle." The unrest among the elves became even greater. "But in the north is the kingdom of the Shadow Elves," shouted a young mother with a small baby in her arms. "So called because the darkness reigns and nobody returns from there alive."

Eyela looked at the young elf with surprise. "It's true," she replied. "I know of these stories also. But I hope that we will not need to ride so far into the north to find Surah. But if we must do so, we are armed against these dangers."

She gave her horse a gentle tap on the right side. This was the sign for departure. The four elves slowly took off, without looking back once because they were afraid that the sight of their beloved Summergreen House would cause them to waver in their decision.

It was midday when the four friends first took a rest. They had a demanding ride behind them because the paths on which they had travelled were narrow and twisting. Only seldom did elves come to this deserted area and they often had the feeling that they were travelling in circles. However, again and again it appeared the friends had made their way back onto the right path.

A lush, green meadow at a clear brook was the right place to take a break and eat something small. The sun was high up in the sky and on the bank flutterlings of all colours flew around. "We'll stay here," decided Eyela and sat under a tree in the shade. "There's water for the horses and we should also take a rest." Falaroy looked around, lost in thought. "This idyll here looks strange to me," he said. "One would think we are on holiday because nothing here suggests a dangerous journey." Sera had to laugh and replied: "Who knows, maybe the whole journey will be just an enjoyable outing. We don't even know if our journey has a purpose." "You're right, sister," Eyela agreed. "But in order to discover that, I've brought this." She took a small glass container from a little bag containing the silver dragon's head, which she had also used already as a light to guide them through the Bannwald forest. "Oh no!" wailed Feya. "Not that again. Who knows what it will bring about this time." "Exactly why I have brought it," said Eyela, looking somewhat amused into the worried eyes of her friend. Sure enough the small dragon's head appeared not to want to change in the slightest. "I don't know if it can be of any use to us," said a disappointed Falaroy, after the elves had waited a while and said nothing. "No, nothing's happening, apart from..." said Sera who stopped and looked around, surprised. "Look, the flutterlings! There are more and more of them and they're flying very anxiously around us and the glass." Eyela had already noticed this and lifted the glass container with the dragon's head up high. She wanted to see what would happen. A great cloud of flutterlings immediately formed, excitedly whirring around Eyela's hand and the glass. A gold-coloured specimen appeared to be particularly attracted to it and placed itself on the silver head of the dragon in the glass container.

Suddenly a loud buzz and whirr could be heard in the air. When the elves looked around, they saw that thousands of flutterlings had ascended into the air from the green of the meadow and had formed a large, thick cloud. The cloud of small insects took hold of the elves, hovered above them and made a deafening noise, so much so that Feya had to press her hands over her ears. The others too found this very eerie. The cloud became thicker, so much so that soon the four elves could hardly make head nor tail of where they were. Everywhere the small insects buzzed with their fast wings. Eyela had long ago let the glass with the dragon's head drop and had covered her ears too. None of them had noticed that the small golden flutterling, as the only one of his kind, still sat motionless on the head of the dragon. The cloud was now already so thick that it was almost impossible to breathe without swallowing an insect in the process. The vast number of tiny wings was blocking out almost all of the sunlight. The four elves tried to drive away the insects but more and more appeared.

At this moment, the little flutterling rose from the head of the dragon and merged with all the others. And as though somebody had given an order, a gentle wind carried the little insects away from the elves.

In the same moment that this happened, the noise was replaced by an unsettling quietness. Eyela and her friends dared once more to open their eyes and to breathe. How their surroundings had changed! There, where the clear brook and the lush meadow had been, was only a deep furrow made from stone and debris. The meadows had been transformed into a barren, steppe-type landscape. Although there should still have been daylight, it was dark because thick clouds, similar to the smoke of a large fire, hung heavy in the air. Only very hazily, like the suggestion of a dark red fire disc, could the sun be made out behind it. "What has happened?" asked Eyela, the first to be able to speak, her voice trembling. "I don't know," replied Falaroy. "It appears to be the same place, although it's hardly recognisable anymore." Feya was afraid. She wished so much that Falaroy would take her in his arms, however it wasn't the right time for such feelings. "Look!" whispered Sera. "There, on the other side of the dry river bed ... something is moving." Eyela also recognised a figure, whose outline seemed to remind her of someone. "Who are you?" she called out bravely. "Show yourself!" Everything was still. Then, however, the elves heard a soft, yet melodic, voice speak. "My child," were the first words. "The dragon and the power of nature, with their thousands of little friends, have led you all to me at this place." "Father!" screamed Eyela. "Is it you who speaks to me? Please come nearer so that we can see you better." "No, dear Eyela," replied the voice softly. "I cannot come to you. Even if you can no longer see the water of the brook, it still separates us. You are here in a place beyond time. Your eyes deceive you because your father is long dead. I am only his spirit who lives in your heart." Sera took hold of Eyela's hand and clasped it tightly. "You speak in riddles. Do you not want to show yourself in the light?" asked Eyela. The figure remained silent, so the King's daughter continued: "My friends and I are looking for Surah, my sister. Can you tell us whether or not she is still alive?" It was a long time before the voice spoke again - this time even quieter than before. "The answers to your questions lie buried in your own heart," replied the shadowy figure once again in riddles. "Right now you are exactly in the place where your sister should be. But there is darkness, drought and uncertainty and it will soon be over the whole of Bayala if the riddle is not solved and the curse is not broken. Take your sister Sera by the hand, close your eyes and let your thoughts go to Surah. Look deep inside yourself, then you will both be shown the way to the place where all riddles will be solved." The last words could hardly be heard as the figure spoke once again: "Sleep now. A dangerous path lies ahead of you all and you need all of your strength." With these words, the shadowy figure disappeared into the darkness and a heavy tiredness overcame the four elves and their horses.

Starry Sky

eya blinked. The sun dazzled her and a soft breeze tickled her nose. She opened her eyes and looked around. Before her the clear brook babbled and small, colourful flutterlings played in the flowers in the meadow where they had slept. There was nothing more to see of the dark, stony drought that had only shortly before surrounded them. On the bank of the brook,

Feya saw the horses, quietly standing beside each other as if nothing had happened. Eyela, Sera and Falaroy awoke now too and looked around. "Did you both have the same curious dream that I did?" asked Feya. "A strange, dark figure spoke to us and the land was gloomy and threatening." Falaroy nodded and said: "I also saw it. However, I'm not sure whether it was a dream or whether it really happened. It seemed to me to be a journey at first, a journey to a place between the real world of Bayala and the world of the elf spirits." Eyela nodded and then said, lost in thought: "*The answers to your questions lie buried in your heart.* The dark figure said that to me." Sera pondered the situation as well, and then asked: "What did he mean when he said that the two of us should hold hands in order to see our innermost thoughts?" She looked at her sister, perplexed. "Let's try it," replied Eyela. "Come, give me your hands... And now we'll close our eyes and think of our sister."

They both closed their eyes and directed their thoughts to Surah. A pleasant warmth developed between their hands, which spread out further with every beat of their pulse. Eyela and Sera noticed how their hands appeared to become undetachable from each other. The warmth flowed into every chamber of their hearts and even filled the space where the dark, the sad and the bleak thoughts were, where the painful memory of their lost sister lay buried. Thoughts turned to images and appeared before the eyes of the two elves...

They saw their father, very old, but happy and dignified as he sat at the dinner table among his family. The dinner table was situated outside, in a pretty glade. To the right of the King sat his wife, the Queen, and to his left, Eyela, the eldest daughter. The table was wonderfully decorated. The plates and tankards were made from precious elf silver and the meals served were of the highest quality, meals only a king could serve his guests. The guests all appeared to be of noble ancestry and wore precious robes. Sera and Surah, the twin sisters, entertained the friends and took part in cheerful discussions.

However, all of a sudden, the sky turned dark and an enormous, black dragon appeared from the sky. The face of the dragon resembled more the one of an old elf woman with pale skin, though its cheeks were scaly and its eyes glassy and green. Before anybody could react, it grabbed Surah. She screamed and struggled, however nothing could be done against the strength of the powerful creature... Surah was snatched upwards by the dragon and carried away. Eyela and Sera wanted to fly after her, but their wings were as if paralysed. They chased after them, screaming, but nothing could be done. The dragon disappeared over the horizon, behind a mountain whose peak resembled a large, stony nest.

The images swam before Eyela's and Sera's eyes and slowly their hands loosened and separated. They opened their eyes. "And, what did you both see?" asked Feya curiously and Falaroy too looked questioningly at the two sisters. Eyela, still slightly stunned by the images, began to explain.

When she came to the end of her description of the vision, Falaroy was the first to speak. "That's a strange story," he said. "What you have seen doesn't correspond to what actually happened to your father and Surah." "That's true," agreed Feya. "The King is already long dead and Surah has never before been seen as an adult elf - assuming she is even still alive." Eyela nodded absently, and then said: "The vision doesn't correspond to reality but we can, however, learn a lot from it. On the one hand, we have seen our father, old, happy and among his friends. We also saw how the future would have been if Surah had not disappeared. This vision of the future has been destroyed with the abduction of my twin sister by the evil dragon. That can only be symbolic, because the actual disappearance happened when she was still a baby." "It also showed us something else though," Eyela put forward after some thought. "We should never have buried the memory of Surah in our hearts, we should have continued searching for her. We have both closed our hearts against her and thus made it impossible for us to find her." A tear rolled down Sera's cheek. "Did you see the mountain with the stony nest?" Eyela asked her sister. "That could be a clue to where our path leads. Father already told me about this place when I was a child. The mountain is called Dragon Cliff and is situated quite a distance west of Oracle Mountain." "Then let's set off for this place," suggested Falaroy. "It is the only clue we have at the moment, we have no other option."

The four elves freshened up at the brook, ate something small and then saddled up the horses. By now it was afternoon and they were eager to cover a good bit of the distance before it was dark.

The horses were strong and travelled very quickly. The roads and paths were now wider and trailed mostly straight through the countryside that now surrounded the friends. There was nothing more to see of the beloved forest and meadow landscape of their home. Gentle hills, like giant waves in an ocean, surrounded the elves, mostly covered with low-growing grass or moss. Here and there, however, this image was broken by bizarre-looking groups of trees which stood in the sea of green like small islands. Large swarms of birds flew swiftly across the sky, almost as if they were fleeing from something. The elves observed this with amazement, without paying particular attention to it. A gentle wind from the south made it a pleasant journey for riding because, on the one hand, it was warm and, on the other hand, the tailwind saved the horses a lot of energy.

The mood of the elves increasingly improved because there was nothing to suggest that any immediate danger lay ahead. Even Feya laughed again and said, winking: "We're riding as fast as the wind. If we didn't have Falaroy in tow, then we'd certainly reach our destination by tomorrow." Sera and Eyela laughed, only Falaroy muttered and, with his horse, placed himself at the front of the group to prove the opposite.

"Three elf women against an elf man – that's not fair!" he shouted, laughing again as well though. "We'll see who's the first to be tired." With his hair blowing in the wind, he took off and Feya followed him. Eyela sensed a slight prick in her heart, but she put it to the back of her mind as she had a more important mission to fulfil and her personal interests, had to take second place.

It was evening and the sun was like a fireball high over the horizon. For a while already the elves had ridden silently beside each other at a light trot. "It's time for us to look for a place to stay the night," said Eyela and the others nodded in agreement. "Look, over there is a small forest," shouted Feya. "We'll be sure to find a nice place to sleep there."
Sure enough, the small forest turned out to be an extremely comfortable place to stay the night. The ground was soft and the branches of the trees hung so low that there was almost as much protection as in a tent. A small source of water provided the necessary refreshment for the horses. Sera knew about the beneficial effect of the water. She collected a few herbs, pressed them left and right on her legs and then let the water flow over her delicate feet. When she was

finished, she covered the legs of her friends in the same way and shortly afterwards the elves felt relaxed.

Soon after the four friends were lying beside each other under a large tree on a soft cover. Through the thick branches of the trees, they could make out the magnificent starry sky. Falaroy was the first to fall asleep and snored softly with his mouth open. Feya giggled, but Sera poked her in her side and said softly: "Go to sleep too. We have a tiring day ahead of us tomorrow."

"Shush!" hissed Eyela just then. "I heard a noise." Feya and Sera perked up their ears and now they could hear it too. It was a soft rustling between the branches of the trees, which appeared to be slowly getting closer. "It will only be a small animal," said Eyela, trying to calm the situation, although her voice revealed she was also a little scared. She stood up and slowly walked towards where the noise was coming from. Cautiously she made her way forward. Eyela pushed a few branches apart and got a fright because she came face to face with two small, glittering eyes. A face, hardly bigger than the width of her hand, looked back at her from the height of her hips. Slowly Eyela's eyes became accustomed to the darkness and she recognised a delicate figure with dainty wings. The skin appeared to be almost transparent and the whole creature shimmered a dark blue. The creature was clothed only in a small, bright dress that looked like a dressing gown. "Who are you?" she asked cautiously. "I hope we haven't disturbed you with our intrusion." The small creature looked shyly to the ground and chuckled. "No...heeheehee...you didn't disturb me at all," it replied with a high voice that sounded something like the twittering of a bird. "I am a Moon Elf and I live here." Eyela was calmer now but at the same time amazed. Her father had often told her bedtime stories about Moon Elves, however she had always considered it to be fantasy. "Then you are a good little elf spirit and the protector of these woods?" The small elf giggled once more as if to say "Yes, that's me." "What's your name?" Eyela asked. In the meantime, Sera and Feya had also joined her and Falaroy was awake too. The Moon Elf's eyes widened. "I don't have a name," she simply said. "Moon Elves don't have names. You can all call me whatever you want." "Well, then I will call you *Starry Sky*, because your eyes sparkle like stars," said Eyela, smiling. "Oh yes, Starry Sky!" exclaimed the small creature excitedly. "I like that." "Come, let's sit and I will tell you what has led us to your forest," suggested Eyela and a few minutes later all four Sun Elves and the Moon Elf were seated comfortably together. Starry Sky listened intently to the stories that Eyela told her. It was a long while before the Moon Elf knew everything. The story was often interrupted by her giggling, which set off Feya and Sera too. Everything appeared to be so easy and happy in this little forest. Eyela did not let that deceive her and told the Moon Elf everything down to the last detail, from the first meeting to the forest they were now in.

"You want to go to Dragon Cliff," said Starry Sky, when the story came to an end and grinned widely again. "I know it well." "You've been there before?" asked Falaroy astonished. "Heehee...yes, but that was a long time ago. I was there before the fog came." "How is that possible?" asked Sera, amazed. "You look too young." "We Moon Elves are a very old people," answered Starry Sky and for a moment her gaze resembled that of an old elf woman. She then giggled again. "Thus we have no names because they mean nothing in never-ending time. If you want...heehee... I will show you all a quicker way to Dragon Rock than the way you intend to go." "That would be a great help, Starry Sky," said Eyela. "However, we must sleep a bit first to conserve our energy." "Good, then I will return again shortly before sunrise," replied Starry Sky. "Have your things ready because when the sun comes up, I will have disappeared... heehee."

The Elf Spirits

long way from the little forest, Surah was also on the move. She had wrapped up warmly, but the icy cold north wind, which blew in her face as she fled, didn't bode well. She asked herself how her small companion endured the cold, nothing appeared to bother it. It flew bravely ahead.

Observed from above, the palace appeared even bigger and Surah was amazed at the mighty effect it had on her, despite the enormous mountains which surrounded it. She caught sight of Shadow Rock, the place of her secret transformations and was happy to have chosen a new path.

Surah and her feathered friend flew in a southern direction, but they did not make good progress as the uneven and stormy wind made flying almost impossible. Furthermore, on this day everything was even more grey and the sky more overcast than usual. The small amount of light that penetrated through the thick wafts of fog was not enough to allow flying. "We won't make it very far," thought Surah, quickly suppressing the thought as she didn't want to give up so soon into the journey.

The small, green bird happily fluttered further, yet after a while its strength appeared to leave it because it flew down towards the ground. Surah followed, even though she didn't understand why.

A short time later, the elf sat on a large stone in the desolate rocky landscape. Her small friend snuggled up to her cold cheek. Surah loved it when the bird was close to her; however, despite the warmth that came from it, she increasingly doubted that it could really help her.

What Surah did not know was that the bird was not tired at all. It had hardly given enough warmth when it flapped from her shoulder and hopped to a large, gnarled tree stump which lay on the rocky ground, not far away from Surah's stone. The elf followed the bird and made a strange discovery. The tree stump lay over an opening in the ground ~ a narrow cave entrance, which appeared to plunge down into the depths below. The entrance to the rocky hole was sharp and jagged so that the entire cave looked like the wide-open mouth of a monster.

Surah shuddered when she saw it; however, it didn't appear to bother the bird because it hopped without hesitation around the tree stump and the opening in the ground. The elf took a stone and dropped it into the hole. She listened to hear the stone bounce so that she could correctly calculate how deep the hole was. She listened intently but there was no sound to be heard. Instead something unexpected happened. Surah all of a sudden felt herself being pulled through the hole in the rock. It developed into a pull that was so strong the decayed wood of the tree stump burst into small pieces and the elf was pulled into the darkness bit by bit. She stumbled, lost her footing and her legs slipped. With a last-ditch effort,

Surah grabbed tightly onto the sharp, jagged opening, yet the pull grew stronger and stronger. "This is where it all ends," thought Surah, before she lost all her strength and was finally pulled down into the cave.

Surah felt herself falling. She tried to flap her wings, however the vertical hole in which she had fallen was too narrow for her even to be able to move. The elf noticed how her clothes on her arms and legs had ripped and she had scraped herself. Thoughts and images flashed before her. Scraps of words darted about in her head. She fell and fell... The darkness that surrounded her robbed her of a sense of space and time. Then, suddenly, Surah noticed how her hair, which had already been thrown wildly upwards from the fall, only now lightly streamed out behind her. Moments later, the individual strands fell back onto her shoulders. Suddenly there was a stillness around her. Surah tried to look around; however, it was so dark that she had not the slightest idea of where she was. Suddenly, she sensed a familiar feeling at her shoulder and her heart leapt. Soft feathers nestled up to her cheek and warmth flowed through her body. Surah noticed how she softly came to the ground, lying on her back, with her arms, legs and wings stretched out. She lay there like that for a while, waiting for her breath to return. She wasn't completely sure if she was alive or already dead, but the wounds on her arms and legs painfully made her realise that she must still be alive.

At this moment, a small hole opened up behind Surah and some light shone in. The elf sat up. Her entire body hurt, however she made a wonderful discovery. Every wound on her body and every bloodied joint immediately healed the minute she encountered her small, green friend. Once again Surah felt a deep sense of gratitude that she had found the magic creature.

Now, as her eyes slowly grew accustomed to the poor light, the elf could see where she was. She stood in a small, cave-type chamber with jagged rock walls, at the end of which a small stone slab was embedded. This had opened a crack and thus allowed some light to enter. Surah grasped the edge of the slab and tried to open it further in order to find out what was behind it. Warm light in all the colours of the rainbow shone towards her. The source was countless small lights at the far end of a large vaulted cellar. Shadowy figures flitted silently through the room, undisturbed by Surah.

The elf took a deep breath and entered the chamber with the lights through the small opening. All of a sudden she knew where she was. The light came from numerous figures made from elf silver, which stood in small wall openings. Surah also recognised that many cave passageways led to the chamber into which the strange shadowy figures disappeared again and again. Without doubt this was the chamber, deep under the ancestral halls of the palace, from which she had taken the dragon figures to her room. But how had she got here? The elf began to realise that the chamber was probably the centre of a large imaginary network of cave passageways which stretched from here out into the whole kingdom.

On the one hand, Surah was happy to be in a place she knew, on the other hand, she was disappointed that she had not yet managed to get the slightest bit away from the palace. She thought about what she should do.

That moment she noticed that she wasn't alone in the chamber. In a dark corner of the vaulted hall she recognised a bright pair of eyes shyly observing her. Cautiously, Surah took a few steps forward. The shadowy figures appeared not to notice at all, but rather flitted further through the chamber or disappeared into the cave passageways. Surah tried to get closer to the shy figure. She thought she now recognised the figure hiding in the far corner better. She guessed it would be an elf sitting on a dog or a wolf, totally transfixed, almost as if it was a statue. Yet Surah was sure that it was not a statue. "Hello, little friend," she called in a low voice, so as not to frighten the spirits. "Who are you? Can you speak?" The small elf creature lifted its head a little. "Of course I can speak," he answered with a voice as if he was talking to a child. "I have been waiting here for you." Surah was amazed. How could it be that somebody was waiting for her here at this place? The previous times that she had been in the vaulted hall she had never noticed anyone, but it had meanwhile become clear to her that someone could be peeping out from the dark cave passages at any time without being discovered. "You've been waiting for me?" she asked, incredulously. "But how is that possible? It is a pure coincidence that I'm here." "It is far from a coincidence," replied the childlike voice. "You are of royal blood and the hall of the dragons, princes and kings draws you magically, just like your little friend the bird." "You are mistaken," answered Surah. "My blood is not at all royal. I am just a poor elf searching for answers. But who are you that you can claim such a thing?" She heard a gentle laugh.

"I am Jaro, the little messenger of the old kings and princes of Bayala," it replied. "My parents died shortly after my birth and I was brought up by the wolves of the forest. Therefore, I know every cave and every shelter." Jaro was silent for a moment, then he continued: "One day I discovered a cave which opened out into this hall. At first, the spirits of the old rulers were angry with me but when they saw that I was still a child and meant no harm to them, they made me their messenger." Surah marvelled at what she heard. "How long have you known this vault here?" she asked. Jaro laughed again softly. "It is some time ago that I was first here," he said. "But that is not important. I have often watched you taking the figures. No elf would ever survive that who was not of royal blood." "It's driving me crazy not knowing who I am!" exclaimed Surah. "Can you not tell me?" "I don't know who you are either," replied Jaro. "But I can help you find out." "Yes, please do!" begged Surah. "I will give you everything that I have." "I do not want gifts from you," said the young elf quietly. He bent forward slightly and whistled loudly between his fingers. The wolf on which he sat reared up slightly, then started running in a circle with the young boy.

The ghostly figures in the room formed a small group and magically transformed themselves. From the black, misty creatures, bright, almost angelic spirits appeared. They appeared transparent and aloof, however, every now and then something could be seen in the bodiless figures that resembled an elf. The vaulted hall was now no longer dark, but had been brightened by the light of the spirits. The young elf with the wolf and the elf spirits formed a circle around Surah and the small bird. Slowly they moved closer, until they could reach for the elf. They plucked at her clothes and at her hair. A curious mumbling filled the stuffy cellar air. Although Surah was afraid, she had no choice but to wait and see what happened. When the creatures closed in on her, another whistle was heard. The wolf and the young elf stood before the large wall opening, as if they were waiting. Surah sensed that she was being lifted up high and countless spirit hands carried her. She felt like she was on a wave made of foam. Now everything happened quickly. The elf realised that she was being carried towards the large wall opening by the hands and would disappear within it. She saw the young boy and the wolf before her, beside her and then again behind her. Now and then she heard a shrill whistle. She was carried through the passageways away from the vaulted hall faster and faster and deeper and deeper into the enormous mountains of the north.

In the Crater of the Volcano

t the same time, Nuray, Ophira, Turag and their followers were riding to the south. Although the dark ruler did not know exactly where the journey would take them, she was sure that the Oracle would provide an answer.

Bilara, the elf sorceress, did not ride at the front at Nuray's side. She stayed a little apart from the small group that had joined them for reinforcement. Nuray was silent. Ophira and

Turag had wrapped scarves around their faces in order not to be totally exposed to the icy wind. The dark ruler knew the way well, for in her youth she had often accompanied her mother on long rides into this area.

The group made good progress, despite the steep rocks and high mountains. The paths through the valleys and the mountain passes were mostly wide and easily accessible. Many of these paths were already very old, for they had been built long ago by the old elf princes of darkness helped by the dragons. Ophira kept straining her eyes looking all around in the hope of spotting Surah somewhere. She felt that Nuray had acted carelessly in letting Surah simply fly off. Ophira was much more mistrustful and feared that the elf with her feathered friend perhaps did have more power than they all supposed. However, try as she might, Ophira could not see Surah anywhere.

As the afternoon wore on, thick fog gathered in the valleys of the Shadow Kingdom. The horses now had to go more slowly, as visibility was deteriorating by the hour. Turag glanced at Nuray from the side and said: "I think we should look around for somewhere to spend the night. When it's dark it will be

bitterly cold and it will be difficulty to find somewhere."
Nuray raised her head and looked at Turag with glassy eyes.
She seemed to be a long way away in her thoughts. She had
been overcome by memories of the time with her mother.
"What...What did you say, Turag?" she stammered. It took a
while before she could think clearly again. "Oh, right, about
somewhere to spend the night. Don't worry. We'll soon be
at a place where we can stay. There's an old volcano crater
near here that my mother once showed me. We'll be safe
there. Above all, it's warm, because the boiling lava is just
below the bottom of the volcano." "When will we get there?"
Turag asked. "The horses are tired, and we're making very
slow progress because of the fog." "It's not much further,"
Nuray reassured him. "Just round a few more bends, then
we'll be there."

The dark ruler was right, for after just a short while Turag
saw a small volcano that could be entered from the north
and the south through two openings in the rock. The inside
of the crater was so large that there was plenty of space for
the whole group, including the horses. From the bottom of
the crater they could feel a pleasant warmth – not too hot,

but just right to make them feel comfortable. Nuray started to spread her blanket for the night. She then sat on a stone, took out the food hamper and had something to eat.

Turag took care of the horses, at the same time talking to Ophira. Nuray wondered what they might be discussing of such importance, but just as she was about to get up and join them, Bilara approached her. "Nuray, I'd like to talk to you," she said softly but resolutely. The dark ruler looked up in astonishment, because it was very seldom that the sorceress would herself seek conversation. "What's troubling you?" asked Nuray, looking at Bilara a little suspiciously from the side. "Nothing's troubling me," replied the sorceress in a fine, but firm voice. "You are the one whose soul seeks fulfilment." Nuray stood up and stared into Bilara's eyes. "What do you mean?" she hissed. "What do you know of me?" Bilara drew back a little, but without breaking eye contact. "I've known you since you were small," the sorceress replied calmly. "You are forgetting that I advised your mother and therefore already knew of Uhara's striving for power. You are her daughter, so of the same flesh and blood." Nuray continued to stare at Bilara's lips as if in a trance. She hesitated one moment, then replied: "You perhaps know more about me than I like. But that's precisely the reason I brought you along on this journey. I want you to help me fulfil the legacy of my mother." Bilara smiled coldly. "The legacy of your mother...," she then said calmly, "...means gaining power over the whole of Bayala." Nuray nodded slowly. "That is what my mother strove for," she replied. "And I will complete it." Bilara now stepped up close to the dark princess and whispered in her ear: "How do you intend to achieve that, my love? You know neither the way, nor the destination." Nuray drew back in fright. Bilara was right, for in principle she really did not know where to start. "Our way leads to Oracle Mountain," she retorted with determination in her voice. "Where, a long time ago, my mother received the words that were to take her to King Baramah's palace. The key to power must be hidden on that magical mountain." "Oracle Mountain, the most sacred place in our kingdom – do you really want to go there?" asked Bilara. Nuray thought she detected a scornful smile on her lips. "The Oracle will not show you the way to power," said Bilara so quietly that certainly nobody else could hear. Nuray looked at her in astonishment. "What do you mean?" she asked, for the dark ruler felt really sure of what she was doing. "The Oracle will not answer your questions, still less give you power over the entire kingdom," replied Bilara self-confidently. "The Oracle is there for all the elves of Bayala. That already proved to be Uhara's undoing when she tried to use the voice for her own ends." Nuray looked at the ground in consternation. She could see that there was some truth in the sorceress's words. "Very well, Bilara," she said after a period of silence. "What do you advise me to do? It was my desire to take you along on this journey and now the day I need your advice has come much sooner than I expected." "There is a place a little to the west of Oracle Mountain," Bilara started. "It is called Dragon Cliff. It is the centre of power in our kingdom, for it is where the mightiest dragons of Bayala once lived. All rulers used to come to the cliff to make their sacrifice. But one day the pact with the dragons was broken and the land became engulfed in fog. The dragons withdrew to the mountains long ago, but the place itself has lost nothing of its might."

Nuray had been listening attentively. She knew Dragon Cliff from many tales and folklore, but she had never realised how important the place was for Bayala. "We are a long way from Oracle Mountain, and even further from Dragon Cliff," the dark ruler observed. "I don't know whether our horses are strong enough for such a journey." Bilara seemed to smile and said: "You forget that I have magic powers. I know a faster way to Dragon Cliff." Nuray pricked up her ears. "A faster way than horses?" she asked incredulously. "Then show me!" "As you wish," replied the sorceress. "Tomorrow morning, before daybreak, we will call all our companions together. I will then show you the fastest way to get there." With these words, Bilara turned and withdrew to sleep.

Nuray spent a restless night, for she could not stop thinking about what the elf sorceress had said. Bilara seemed to be clever, but deep down the dark ruler doubted her words.

As night slowly turned to morning, she rose and awoke all her companions. It had not escaped Ophira that Nuray and the sorceress had had a long discussion. She was suspicious of what would happen next, for Bilara's magic power was a thorn in her side.

They all gathered in the middle of the crater, where Bilara had been standing almost motionless for some time. In her hand she held a crystal ball, into which she was staring as if spellbound. Nuray stood beside her looking into the astonished and curious faces of the gathered elves. "We have come here together because Bilara wants to show us a way," she started. "A way that will take us to our destination as fast as possible." The Shadow Elves seemed amazed. "What is our destination, then?" asked Turag. "We don't even know yet exactly where we're going. Didn't we want to go to Oracle Mountain?" "That was my original plan," replied Nuray. "But Bilara has shown me that I could be mistaken. Our new destination is Dragon Cliff." "Dragon Cliff!" shouted Ophira, her voice quivering. "Since the fog came over the land and the dragons disappeared forever, it has become a dangerous place. It is said that Dragon Cliff is haunted by the spirits of dead elf princes." Nuray looked at her aunt angrily. "I will not force anybody to come who doesn't wish to," she replied. She then turned to the sorceress and said: "Bilara, now show us the way that will take us there."

The elf sorceress seemed no longer to be aware of what was happening around her. She was continually murmuring unintelligible words and staring into the crystal ball. The ground started to tremble slightly. Bilara's words were now getting louder and more penetrating, and with every sentence the trembling increased. Suddenly, at the far side a large chunk of the crater bottom fell away into the depths. Glowing, red masses of lava were visible, and the Shadow Elves drew back a few steps in fear. Larger and larger pieces of ground broke away and fell into the hot masses of molten rock. "What are you doing?" shouted Nuray in shock, but Bilara seemed to hear nothing. Ophira too had drawn back a few steps. "Look, how peculiar!" she called. "It looks like the lava is flowing down into the depths on steps." Meanwhile, Turag had also noticed this fact. "Steps glowing with fire... if that's our path, then count me out," he observed soberly. "We would burn up after just a few steps." Bilara had meanwhile fallen silent and now raised her hands imploringly. When she heard Turag's words, she turned to him: "You fool!" she hissed. "Have you forgotten who I am? If you want to reach your destination fast, you have to go through the fire. It's the shortest way. So that you won't burn, each of you must touch my crystal ball for one moment. That will give you protection until you get to Dragon Cliff." Turag remained silent, but a strange smile appeared on his lips.

Nuray looked at the others. "Well, who of you is coming?" she asked, trying to hide the fact that she too was afraid.

Three of the Shadow Elves who had accompanied the princess of darkness immediately declined. Under no circumstances would they go into the fire, but wanted to ride back to the palace. The others seemed undecided. "Very well, as you wish," shouted Nuray in anger. "Just ride home then. But take our horses with you, for we must follow this path without them."

She stepped up to Bilara and touched the crystal ball with her hands. An ice-cold shudder ran through her body. The other elves now approached slowly and, one after another, touched the ball. Then, Bilara took Nuray by the hand and they walked together towards the lava steps. Ophira, Turag and the Shadow Elves who were brave enough to join them followed. The sorceress and the dark princess now made their first step onto the lava steps. To her surprise, Nuray felt none of the incredible heat that must have prevailed. Neither did she burn her feet. The elf sorceress and the dark ruler now went down the glowing steps into the depths.

Turag

urag and Ophira followed Nuray and Bilara, accompanied by the other Shadow Elves. The walls beside the lava steps seemed like waterfalls of liquid fire. The elf sorceress went ahead, but what amazed Ophira was that Bilara did not even look around, as if she experienced such an adventure every day. The other elves, apart from Turag and Nuray, seemed full of fear. "No wonder the sorceress feels fine here," thought Ophira to herself. "After all, she lives in a volcano. Who knows what witchcraft she gets up to down there night and day."

Turag gave the impression that the fiery surroundings did not cause him too much trouble. Ophira found his behaviour a little odd, but she could not figure out what troubled her about it. The group of Shadow Elves descended deeper and deeper into the mountain. The lava around them became more liquid, and there were large swirls of fire on the side walls. After the elves had been going for some while, the steps gradually became less steep, until after a while they completely disappeared, leaving a straight, flat fiery passage. The passage soon stopped at a dead-end, where Nuray and the other Shadow Elves discovered a lava flow.

Bilara raised her hand to ask for silence. "This is *the Great River* of Fire," she said. "It is the mightiest underground lava flow in Bayala, and extends from the far north to the deep south. Its branches lead to almost everywhere in our kingdom." Nuray was astonished and asked: "You mean this river could even take us to Dragon Cliff?" Bilara nodded. "But how?" asked Nuray uneasily. "We can't swim through the fire." The sorceress shook her head. "No, nobody can swim in this river," she said. "But look." She pointed to the rear left corner of the fiery passage through which the group had come to the river. "Over there are three boats made of elf ice. With them we can travel on the River of Fire." The Shadow Elves looked in amazement to where she was pointing at the boats. And indeed they could make out three simple shapes that resembled the rump of a small ship.

They gave off a bluish shimmer and were so transparent that at first sight you could hardly see them. "Elf ice is so strong that no power in this world can make it melt," explained Bilara. "But be careful! Our journey may be very rough. The nearer we approach Dragon Cliff the faster the river will become. So hold on tight!"

Ophira did not like the idea of being so totally at the mercy of the sorceress. But at the moment she had no choice but to set off on the journey on the River of Fire with the others. Turag and two other male Shadow Elves pulled the boats out from the corner. The elf ice felt cold and smooth, but not so icy that you could not sit in it. Nuray now asked them all to get in. She herself and Bilara got into the first boat, Turag and Ophira got into the second, and the remaining companions got into the last and largest boat.

A short while later, the three boats were floating down the river. The current was strong right from the start, so the group made rapid progress. Bilara stood at the bow of her boat and held up her hands imploringly. She had closed her eyes and was again murmuring words that Nuray had never heard before.

The dark ruler kept looking around in awe, for the river seemed to be getting wider as the journey progressed. However, the walls enclosing the river were now no longer only of lava, but now and then you could also see large rocks that defied the might of the fire.

Bilara opened her eyes again and sat down beside Nuray. "Hold on tight!" she said. "We will soon be going even faster, and if you don't watch out you'll soon be thrown overboard." The elf ice did not provide much opportunity for a firm grip, but Nuray understood and tried to hold on wherever she could.

The boats were now moving faster and faster. The increasing waves of hot lava were now powerfully driving the boats downstream. "Bilara, that witch!" thought Ophira. "She'll lead us all to our deaths. Who knows who she's in league with and what her intentions are!" She could not think any more, for the ride had now become so fast that the travellers all had to concentrate their efforts on not being thrown overboard. The individual rock and lava formations were now a vague outline, flying past the elves in a red, yellow and orange blur. Nuray felt as if she was being shot through a great fiery pipe and hoped deep down that they would not be smashed on a rock. But nothing of the sort happened.

When the Shadow Elves were moving so fast that they had to hold their breath, there was suddenly a bright flash. Nuray was almost blinded for a few moments, but when her eyes became reaccustomed to normal brightness, she looked around in amazement. The side walls, which had just been glowing red with the lava, were now covered with moss-like growth in all conceivable shades of green. The River of Fire was now more like a wide river with dark-blue water on which the boats gently floated along. Nuray looked at Bilara questioningly. "Don't be deceived, Nuray," she said, because she could guess the dark ruler's thoughts. "We are still travelling at great speed, but your senses are no longer able to follow what is happening before your eyes. You therefore see this illusion that we have almost stopped still in the water." The other elves were also looking around uneasily. Ophira still did not trust the spookiness and wanted to say something, but Turag grabbed her arm and stopped her. "Wait," he whispered. "We can't do anything at the moment, and it would be foolish to annoy Bilara while we're still in her hands."

The river journey continued, and Nuray was relieved that they were no longer moving at a breakneck speed, but the boats were now apparently floating along gently on the smooth, dark water.

"Where are we now?" she asked the elf sorceress. "And when will we reach our destination, Dragon Cliff?" "Where we are exactly I cannot tell you as long as we are under the illusion," replied Bilara. "But I think we will reach our destination soon." "That's impossible!" shouted Nuray flabbergasted. "Oracle Mountain is many days' ride from the palace, and it's probably even further to Dragon Cliff." "You underestimate the power of magic," replied Bilara. "Even though you yourself have experienced it, when you went to Oracle Mountain with the help of the dragon mist, and returned on the clear river." "How do you know that story?" asked Nuray suspiciously, but Bilara just smiled and said: "I saw you when you were washed up on the river bank. The rest I could figure out." Nuray turned round to Turag and Ophira. She wanted to see their reaction to the sorceress's reply. For they must have heard the conversation, the boats were so close together. But Turag just looked down, and it was not clear whether he had heard anything. However, Ophira's eyes glared with anger because of what the sorceress knew. But she said nothing, so Nuray too let matters rest.

Nothing more was said for a while, then Bilara spoke: "Watch out now, for we'll soon be at our destination. As soon as our actual speed is slower, the illusion will disappear and the real lava flow will reappear. So hold on tight!"

As if by magic, there was another bright flash, this time combined with a deafening rushing and hissing noise. Red hot waves rolled one over another and the walls were again like waterfalls of liquid fire. Nuray's hands gripped the boat; she was afraid she might fall into the lava. Luckily the ride soon became smoother and the danger seemed to be past. The river became narrower and the walls now came in closer from the sides. Bilara turned round to the Shadow Elves and exclaimed: "We have reached our destination. The end of our journey is just ahead. Dragon Cliff is directly above us." "Then let us steer the boats to the riverbank," said Turag. "We've been on the river long enough."

Turag, Ophira and the other Shadow Elves went ashore. Now only Bilara and Nuray remained in their boat. Bilara also got out, and Nuray too wanted to go on land, but Turag held her back. "Not you, my princess!" he shouted, and all of a sudden his voice sounded very threatening. "Your journey ends here." Nuray stared at him in disbelief. "What's the meaning of this, Turag! How dare you speak to me in such a tone?" she exclaimed, her eyes glaring dangerously. "Let me on land at once." Nuray stood up and wanted to push Turag aside, but he made no attempt to give way. "No, Nuray," he said firmly. "As I said, your journey ends here. Listen carefully to what I have to tell you." His voice now sounded deeper and even more threatening. "I am Uhara's younger brother and your uncle," he started. "Everybody thought I was dead, and they even dedicated a room to me in the ancestral halls." "My...my...uncle?" Nuray stammered full of horror. "But ... how is that possible?" "Your mother and I once separated in a dispute, for she claimed the whole kingdom for herself," Turag continued. "One dark night, I had to flee the palace in order to prevent myself being killed, and I was able to trick Uhara into believing that I really was dead. But I lived on in the dark caves in the Shadow Kingdom. From a distance, I watched Uhara make you ruler in my place." Turag clenched his fists, shouting: "But I will now be the one to take your place and rule over all of Bayala! A long time ago, before

I returned to you in the palace, I met somebody who took me in. Since that day, we have together forged this plan." Bilara stepped up to Turag's side. "It is thus," the sorceress confirmed. "I found Turag when he was freezing and starving, so I took care of him. Uhara's power had long been a thorn in my side. So I looked after Turag in my crater until he was again strong enough to return to you in the palace." "Do you remember the day I was standing before your gate?" Turag asked Nuray. "You treated me like a beggar. Only over the years did you start to accept me as your servant, and you then made me your army commander. But now fate has changed." Nuray, shocked and worn out, dropped down. She found it hard to order her thoughts. Memories flashed through her head. She wanted to say something but the words stuck in her throat. Bilara stepped up to the boat and said: "The time has now come. The age of Turag, the ruler, and his companion Bilara, the elf sorceress, is starting. And you are doomed." She gave the boat a push with her foot so that it drifted back into the River of Fire and shouted: "Soon the magic power of the crystal ball will wane and the flames will engulf you!" The boat quickly moved away from the bank. Nuray screamed, but Turag and Bilara had already turned to the other elves, who stepped back in fear. Even Ophira thought it wiser to say nothing but to accept fate. She remembered the day she noticed the snake bracelet, one of the princely symbols, on Turag's arm. That, she now realised, was why he could go to the ancestral halls without coming to any harm.

"Who of you will come with us?" asked Turag gruffly, looking at the elves challengingly. "We have arrived at Dragon Cliff."
Ophira and the other elves looked at each other, but they all realised that they were powerless against Turag's might and Bilara's magic. So they meekly followed.

The Sun on the Horizon

yela awoke with a start. Her heart was racing. Something must have happened, for she was overcome with an unknown fear. Beside her lay Feya, Sera and Falaroy, fast asleep. It was still dark in Starry Sky's little forest, but the time of the meeting with the Moon Elf could not be too far off. She looked around. As if in answer to her call, at that moment she glimpsed the shining eyes looking out from behind the nearest bush.

"Wake your companions. It's time to go," whispered Starry Sky when she was standing right beside Eyela. The king's daughter took a blade of grass and tickled her friends' noses. Falaroy sneezed. This woke Feya and Sera, and just a little later the four had packed their things on the horses and were ready to follow the little Moon Elf. Starry Sky led them to a little glade in the forest. Nothing about the place seemed special, only the arrangement of the trees at the edge of the glade was unusual, because, from above, the space in the middle covered with low grass was an exact square.

"Come," said Starry Sky. "We must sit exactly in the middle." The little creature giggled again, which made Feya start giggling too. Starry Sky had brought along a fine piece of cloth that was now spread out on the ground. Eyela was amazed by the magnificent motifs depicted on the cloth. It was divided into four equal areas, on each of which there was artistic embroidery. One image was of a large dragon sitting majestically on a mountain peak with its wings spread. The second motif showed the face of a happy young elf girl, who had decorated her hair with colourful garlands of flowers. The third image depicted Oracle Mountain glowing in the evening sun, and the final motif showed a large stone pyramid hidden among trees.

Starry Sky noticed how the four elves admired the magnificent cloth, and proudly ran her hand over it. "This cloth is the treasure of this forest", the Moon Elf explained. "Every little forest guarded by a Moon Elf in this area has such a treasure." She giggled again. "Heeheehee.. it was made a very long time ago by my ancestors when they came to this forest," Starry Sky explained merrily. "Three of the motifs are just for decoration, but one has a special significance." Eyela looked at the motifs more closely. "Is it the one with the image of Oracle Mountain?" she asked. "After all, it is the centre of our kingdom." Starry Sky clutched her face with her hands. "No, no, no...!" exclaimed the Moon Elf. "That's just a pretty country scene. Take a closer look. You should recognise it." The four friends now tried to discover the special image together. "The pyramid," said Sera pensively after a while. "It's a similar pyramid to the one we discovered during our adventure in the Bannwald forest. I don't have pleasant memories of that time." The Moon Elf nodded eagerly. "Well spotted!" she exclaimed. "The pyramids are what links all the little forests in our kingdom with the great Bannwald forest. We are all connected to each other through them." Feya felt a shudder down her back when she thought of the impenetrable Bannwald forest. She furtively glanced at Falaroy to see whether he too was afraid, but the young elf just sat there listening to Starry Sky.

"But there's no pyramid here," Sera commented. "What do you mean, the pyramids link the forests with each other?" The Moon Elf stood up and walked slowly round the companions and their horses. "I will explain," Starry Sky started. "Bayala has had many kings and princes who ruled over their individual kingdoms. Whenever a ruler died, the elf spirits sent out a messenger to plant trees that would grow to form a little forest. That's why we have so many little forests. The elf spirits themselves still live today in the great Bannwald forest, and as you've already been there you will surely have heard them whispering and mumbling." The four elves flinched at the thought that the noises they had heard in the forest were the sound of spirits. Starry Sky continued: "But that's not all. A stone pyramid was dedicated to each of the deceased rulers as an eternal symbol of former power." "The pyramid in the Bannwald forest – it bore the symbol of our fallen kingdom," Eyela remembered. Starry Sky looked at the king's daughter in awe. "Then your father must have been a great king," she said, clapping her hands. "Only the most illustrious rulers get a pyramid in the Bannwald forest and may join the elf spirits."

Now Falaroy spoke, as he was becoming a little impatient. "You still haven't told us where there's supposed to be a pyramid here," he said. "I can't see one anywhere." Starry Sky giggled. "Heeheehee... you're sitting in the middle of it," replied the Moon Elf with a cheeky wink. "You're just not able to see the pyramid." The four friends looked around in surprise, but, try as they might, they could see nothing that remotely resembled a pyramid.

"I think you're having fun with us," retorted Falaroy a little annoyed. "But we have no time for jokes, for we are looking for Surah." The Moon Elf suddenly became very serious, and for a moment her little face again took on the expression of an old woman. "Jokes? I would never make jokes," said Starry Sky. "Not about the legacy of the old kings. That would be much too dangerous." "Where is the pyramid, then?" Eyela now also asked. "Show us the pyramid so that we know you are telling us the truth." The Moon Elf looked from one to the other, and then said: "Look at this glade. It forms an exact square. That's the outline of the base of the pyramid. The walls rise steeply at the edge of the forest, but they are only visible for just a brief moment during the day. That is when the horizon divides the rising sun into exactly two halves. Then the pyramid is visible for a short time." "It will soon be sunrise," said Feya, pointing to the horizon, above which the red sky of dawn was starting to become visible. Starry Sky again clutched her face with her hands.

"Oh, we mustn't lose any more time!" the little creature exclaimed. "Take the little silver dragon's head and place it exactly in the centre of the cloth. The moment the pyramid becomes visible, drop a little of the elixir that I am about to give you onto the dragon's head. It was brewed by the Moon Elf in the northernmost little forest of our kingdom from the mushrooms that grow there and will help the little dragon's head to take you there. The little forest is not far from Dragon Cliff. You must complete the remaining journey yourselves." Eyela's distrust was aroused. "What do you know of the little dragon's head?" she asked.

The Moon Elf looked to the ground in embarrassment. "Baramah was a great king," Starry Sky then said. "But far away in the north, deep below the stony earth, there is another place where the elf spirits are at home. There they would never accept your father. So somebody must have given him the little dragon's head." Now Eyela was surprised. "You know my father! It's from you that he got the silver dragon's head!" she exclaimed. "That means that all this is thanks to you..." Starry Sky interrupted her. "Whether I know your father or not, the sun is about to rise. Here, take this small flask and drop a little of the elixir onto the dragon's head," said the Moon Elf hastily. "I will leave you now, for I must be at another place before the sun rises."

Suddenly the Moon Elf vanished as if swallowed up by the earth. "Starry Sky!" called Eyela. "Where are you? I wanted to ask you something else about my father!" But the Moon Elf had disappeared.

"Look!" shouted Falaroy. "The sun is rising." The first narrow strip of yellow sunlight was already visible. Eyela hurriedly took out the little dragon's head that she fortunately always carried with her. She placed it in the centre of the cloth. The four Sun Elves then eagerly awaited the moment when the disc of the sun would be divided in the exact centre. Eyela held the flask with the elixir open in her hand.

When the moment came and exactly half of the sun was above the horizon, something strange happened. At the forest edge, stony walls suddenly rose into the sky and met to form a point. This all happened so fast that Eyela almost dropped the flask in fright. But at the last moment, just before the pyramid was complete, she let a few drops fall onto the dragon's head. The top of the pyramid closed and it grew dark. None of the Sun Elves dared to say anything. Feya took hold of Sera's hand and clasped it tightly. Luckily the little dragon's head slowly started to glow red, so a short while later the friends at least had some light.

"The little head is shining. What luck!" Falaroy was the first to find his words. "It already served us once before as a guiding light. Maybe this time too it will help us to find the right path." "Look!" Eyela now cried. "The grass we were sitting on has vanished, and the cloth is gone, too. Everything around us has turned to stone." "The whole interior looks almost the same as the pyramid in the Bannwald forest," observed Sera. "Just the little fountain is missing, and the big dragon statue from which the white mist flowed." "I think you are mistaken," Eyela objected. "I think I can make out a dragon right at the top." In fact there really was a dragon holding on to the top of the pyramid with its strong legs and sharp claws. When she looked up Feya screamed, and the others also got a fright when they saw the great dragon. "It looks almost the same as the dragon on Starry Sky's cloth," whispered Sera. "I just hope it doesn't harm us." At that moment, the dragon let go, and as it dropped it opened its wings. Now that the four friends could see its whole body, they noticed that it had eight legs and its long tail was divided into two at the end. They jumped up and wanted to run to safety, but there was no place in the pyramid where they could hide. The dragon grabbed the elves and their horses and clutched them tightly in its claws. Eyela struggled and tried to free herself, but against the might of the huge animal she was powerless. The dragon flew up, smashed through the top of the pyramid and flew away. The pyramid silently crumbled, and a little while later it was no more to be seen.

The dragon flew up into the sky, but insofar as Eyela was able to recognise anything, the landscape below them had already changed completely. Mountain peaks poked through the mist, and it was considerably colder than just a short time ago in Starry Sky's little forest.

The dragon now flew down, went through the wall of mist and finally landed among high trees in a glade, similar to the one where the elves had seen Starry Sky. The giant animal let the four friends and their horses go and flew off.

The Wall of Mist

yela had to gather herself before she was able to think straight. Her whole body was trembling. The place where the Sun Elves now found themselves was not only much colder than Starry Sky's little forest, the dragon had also given her a great fright.

Feya, Falaroy and Sera also slowly got to their feet. The horses were nervous and were walking round in confusion. Fortunately, however, they had not suffered any injury when the dragon had seized them and carried them away.

Falaroy looked around uneasily. "I hope Starry Sky wasn't wrong," he said, shivering. "This place is much less cosy than the Moon Elf's little forest and I can't tell whether we've really come closer to our destination or not." The other Sun Elves also seemed to be at a loss. "It's misty here, but still bright enough to fly," Sera remarked. "One of us could fly through the mist up into the sky. There we'd be able to get a better view of where we are."

The four friends were silent. None of them really wanted to fly through the mist, because who could say how dangerous that would be? Neither did the Sun Elves all want to fly together, for there was no point in all of them exposing themselves to danger.

"I'll do it," said Feya suddenly, her voice trembling slightly. "I'll fly up and check out the surroundings." Eyela looked at her in surprise. "No, Feya, that's not a good idea," she said. "Falaroy or I will go and have a look around from above." "No," objected Feya, gathering all her courage. "Since we set off I've done nothing of any use. The moment has now come for me to bear some responsibility." Eyela smiled. "Well, OK," she said. "If it is your wish, so be it. We would all be very grateful if you took on this task." Falaroy seemed worried, but said nothing, for he knew how important it was for Feya to face the danger.

A short time later Feya was ready to set off. She had put on some warmer clothing, for the mist was clammy and damp. The elf looked around once more, and her gaze rested for a moment on Falaroy's fine face. Then she flew off.

Feya quickly reached the highest treetops, where the mist now settled like a wall. Despite her warm clothes she was shivering, for the dampness penetrated all her garments. Soon she could see nothing, everything was white before her eyes. Feya lost her sense of space, soon she no longer knew which way was up or down. Sometimes she did not even know if she was flying or just hovering on the spot flapping her wings helplessly.

She grit her teeth. This wall of mist would have to end sometime, for the eight-legged dragon had flown through it when he set the elves down on the ground. Feya painfully realised that her strength could not compare to that of a giant dragon.

The elf was thinking of giving up, but the moment she lost all hope she thought she could see a faint gleam of light through the white mist. The elf flew towards the light and her eyes had not deceived her. Feya's heart leapt as the hope arose in her that she could still overcome the wall of mist. With every beat of her wings the light grew brighter, and soon she flew out of the mist and the sky opened up before her.

In her joy, Feya flew a few large loops before she remembered her task. Her eyes gradually grew accustomed to the brightness of the sun shining above the thick blanket of cloud. She looked around. At some distance, Feya could see a high mountain, which doubtless had to be Oracle Mountain. Every elf in Bayala, including Feya, knew its distinctive form. When the elf looked in the opposite direction, however, she saw something else that fascinated her much more. Directly before her, less than half a day's ride away, she could make out the jagged peak of a mountain that unmistakably had to be Dragon Cliff. Feya saw the stony nest that rose bizarrely above the steep rocks to the mountain summit. Some other mountain peaks also rose above the blanket of mist and cloud. Feya did not want to keep her friends waiting any longer, however, for she had seen enough. "So Starry Sky was not lying," thought Feya, amazed at how incredibly fast their journey had been with the help of the stone pyramid. But what worried Feya was how she was to return through the mist to her friends.

Then a thought struck her. If she just stopped flapping her wings, she would surely just drop. So she would fall right through the wall of mist, as the mist could not stop her. She just had to start beating her wings in time as soon as she had penetrated the mist, otherwise she would crash to the ground. Feya realised that her plan was dangerous, but the danger was more acceptable to her than flying blindly back through the impenetrable mist.

She carefully looked around once more, for she wanted to take good note of the direction of Dragon Cliff. Then, without further consideration, she drew in her wings to her side and let herself drop.

She felt herself entering the mist and again felt the cold, but she did not waver. Once again, she felt she was losing all sense of orientation and her eyes vainly sought to see something. The fall wind pulled at her hair and clothing, but Feya was glad of this for she could be certain that she was leaving the mist behind.

Suddenly she felt a strong pain in her left thigh. From one moment to the next, the mist had disappeared, and Feya saw that she was falling into the top of a tall tree. She quickly opened her wings. On all sides, branches and leaves lashed her body. Just in time, before she crashed to the ground, Feya managed to catch her fall with her wings.

Eyela, Sera and Falaroy had been worried about their friend. When they saw Feya falling through the top of the tree and then hit the ground hard, they feared the worst. "Feya!" shouted Eyela, running across to her friend. The others followed.

The king's daughter anxiously bent down to the injured elf. "Thank heaven, you're alive," she shouted in relief when she saw Feya open her eyes. She carefully helped her friend to her legs. Sera examined the injuries on Feya's arms and legs. "You were lucky," she then remarked. "Just a few cuts. They will soon heal." The injured elf now seemed a little calmer and was gradually getting over her fright. "I'll make you some herbal bandages, then you won't feel any more pain," Sera suggested, but Feya objected. "No, the injuries aren't so bad," she said. "We have no time to lose, for I have seen Dragon Cliff. It is not far from here. With the horses, we'll be there before dark." Surprised, Eyela looked at her friend with worry. "So we really have got to the place we wanted," she stated. "Now we'll soon find out if we're on the right track." She then said to Feya: "But first you must rest and see to your wounds before we ride." "Thank you, but it's not necessary," Feya again replied. "We can set off at once. I don't want us to be late. Who knows whether Surah is in great danger, if she really is still alive. Let's pack our things and get moving." "Very well, as you wish," Eyela replied after a little hesitation. "We'll ride on to Dragon Cliff. My intuition tells me that something is going to happen today. I just hope we are strong enough."

The horses had meanwhile calmed down, so the four elves were able to pack their things and load them. Falaroy carefully helped Feya mount her horse, as her arms and legs were still hurting. "We must ride in that direction," she said without hesitation, and the group set off.

Deep down in the cave passages inside Dragon Cliff, Turag and Bilara were gradually going up with their companions. The sorceress's crystal ball was shining so brightly that they could easily see their way. The group had already left the molten lava masses behind. Instead, they were now struggling through black volcanic rock and grey ash toward the mountain summit.

Surah, meanwhile, was still being carried on the hands of the elf spirits. The surging wavelike motion had some time back already put her in a state of trance, so she no longer clearly perceived where she was and who her companions were.

Everything was rushing by so fast. Surah saw passageways opening up at the sides and little halls through which she was carried in haste. Now and again, Jaro appeared beside her and tried to talk to her, but in Surah's head the words became jumbled and formed absurd sentences and expressions. "King of Bayala's daughter," she thought she heard several times, and then: "Back off...before you fall into the depths... take the book...then the mirror...until the bird dies..."

The elf tried to listen carefully, but her mind was too confused and the rushing noise caused by the shadowy figures was too loud for her to understand the meaning of the words.

The Sun Elves were making slow progress with their horses. The mist continually obstructed their vision, so they had to be careful not to lose their direction. On account of the humidity the soil in this area was very soft, and the horses' hooves kept getting stuck.

Finally, after Eyela had started to fear they would not reach Dragon Cliff that day, she felt their path slowly starting to wind upwards. Soon they reached the thickest wall of mist at the foot of the mountain. "Be very careful," Eyela warned her friends. "Keep looking to the ground and try to keep the path in your sights. Let's keep close together so we don't lose each other." They thus gradually struggled up along the narrow path at the foot of Dragon Cliff.

Sera and Surah

urag breathed heavily, for the ascent through the labyrinth of caves inside Dragon Cliff was steep and difficult. The group of Shadow Elves around Ophira, who were following him, also had to struggle. Only Bilara seemed to advance without effort, almost as if she was being pulled up by her crystal ball. Ophira had meanwhile composed herself a little and sorted her thoughts. She could not understand how Turag could be

Uhara's brother, but she did not doubt the truth of his words for one moment. Now that she knew, she could see the similarity between the black elf and his sister. Ophira, who herself was only Nuray's aunt twice removed, saw that her own quest for power had failed. She cursed silently to herself. What more could she do other than join Turag and Bilara, just as she had previously joined Nuray?

Bilara, the elf sorceress, stopped for a moment and turned to the other Shadow Elves. "We are not far now from the top of Dragon Cliff," she said. "Can you hear the noise rising from the many caves and passageways? This is the place of the elf spirits. So do not look around when we walk the last part and do not answer the murmuring and screaming voices. Whoever attracts the anger of the elf spirits is lost." Turag shuddered at the thought that there were spirits here, but he walked on, obstinately staring at the ground, behind the elf sorceress.

Surah noticed how the waves of the spirits' hands were becoming calmer. She was again able to think clearly and looked around. The wave of the white shadowy figures continued to carry her through narrow cave passageways, but they seemed to be approaching the destination as the journey was becoming noticeably slower.

Jaro was riding on his wolf at the front as if on the crest of a wave. Occasionally he looked round to see whether Surah had fully recovered her senses. "We'll soon be where I wanted to take you," the elf boy said to Surah. "Then you must continue alone, for neither the elf spirits nor I can help you any further." "Where have you brought me?" Surah asked. "The place is called Dragon Cliff," Jaro replied. "Beside Oracle Mountain, it is the most important place in our kingdom, for there the fates of several rulers of Bayala were sealed. Because of the mist, the mountain has almost been forgotten, but now a new age may be starting, for Surah, the king's daughter, is returning." Surah still did not understand what Jaro meant by calling her the king's daughter. However, she had meanwhile gained confidence in the boy and just let everything happen.

A little later, the cave passage opened up into a small chamber whose walls seemed to be made of coarse igneous rock. Several passageways opened into this chamber, some large, others very narrow.

There was a whistle and Jaro raised his hand. Surah felt the spirits carefully let go and place her on her feet. "We will leave you now," said the elf boy gently. "Can you see the opening at the far end of the chamber? Go through and face your destiny. Today you will find the answers to the questions that are burning in your soul."

There was another whistle, and in the same way that the shadowy spirits had turned into figures of light, they now again became dark, bodiless beings. They quickly disappeared into the cave passages, taking Jaro and his wolf with them.

The Sun Elves and the king's daughter Eyela were making but slow progress in the thick mist. They had to take great care not to lose sight of each other. Time and again the path forked, and sometimes the way the Sun Elves took ended in nothing, which meant they had to ride back.
Finally, when Eyela almost wanted to turn round, the mist started to clear a little. She looked up, and above she could make out the first patches of a clear sky. A short time later, the friends had finally made it, and the mist lay at their feet like a white sea. Dusk was already approaching and

the paths were becoming visibly narrower. "Look up there," said Eyela to her friends. That's the summit of Dragon Cliff." Impressed by the jagged rocks and the great dragon's nest made of stone, the friends slowly rode on.

Bilara was startled when a whole horde of dark shadowy figures crossed her cave passage on the way to the summit of Dragon Cliff. Among them, she thought she could make out a figure resembling an elf and a wolf-like animal. "I don't like this," she said to Turag. "Some kind of magic is going on here. We must hurry."
Bilara hastened up the steep cave passage and Turag tried to follow her.

Surah went through the opening that Jaro had shown her at the end of the chamber and into the open air. She looked around and saw to her surprise that she was on the summit of a mountain. The rocks were in the shape of a giant dragon's nest and several cave passages penetrated into the depths of the mountain.
The sun was just going down over the horizon in the mist, and a light breeze was starting up. "Where's my friend, the little

bird?" Surah thought. Without the bird she felt vulnerable. "The last time I saw it was in the great ancestral hall – where I met Jaro." She sighed. Slowly she went across the stony nest to the edge of Dragon Cliff.

The four Sun Elves had meanwhile dismounted their horses a little below the dragon's nest. A small plateau with rocky ground seemed ideal to tie the horses and to continue on foot. Sera looked up trying to decide which path they should follow. "I fear the ascent is too dangerous," she said to the others. "Directly beneath the summit, the rock falls away almost vertically." She stopped suddenly, for she saw the dark silhouette of an elf against the evening sky. "Look!" shouted Sera. "There's somebody up there!" The others had meanwhile also seen the figure at the edge of Dragon Cliff. "Careful," whispered Eyela excitedly. "We are at a place ruled by spirits. We should be cautious in what we do." "The figure doesn't seem like a ghost to me," Falaroy remarked. "It is more like the figure of an elf girl." Eyela had to agree with the elf man, for the appearance did not seem especially ghostlike. She gathered her courage and called out as loud as she could: "Hello, you up there! Who are you? Show us who you are!"

Surah hesitated. She too had already noticed the group of elves and their horses, but who knew whether they had sinister intentions? Surah considered what she should answer, but she felt uneasy about disclosing her name straight away. "I have come from the north," she therefore called out in reply. "Please tell me first who you are!" "I am Eyela, the Sun Elf and daughter of King Baramah!" the king's daughter identified herself. "And this is my sister Sera and my friends Feya and Falaroy." The mention of Sera's name caused a hefty stab in Surah's heart. She stumbled and almost fell. "I am Surah!" she then called. "I have come from the Shadow Kingdom to discover who I am."

"Surah!" cried Sera, and her heart beat wildly. "My twin sister! You're alive!" Eyela felt her legs go weak, and Falaroy and Feya were also overwhelmed by what they had heard. Surah was staggered at these words. She felt herself losing grip and falling backwards, but two strong arms caught her. The black shape of a large elf man stepped up to the edge of the cliff, the defenceless Surah in his arms. "So you have found each other," Turag's deep voice resounded threateningly from the top of the cliff. "But unfortunately it will also be your last meeting." The elf sorceress Bilara stepped up to his side. "Sera and Surah, the twin sisters. One was kidnapped when the Oracle was betrayed by Uhara. Now the day has come to reunite you." She then laughed, which made the Sun Elves shudder. "Let Surah go!" shouted Eyela bravely. "You have no right to keep her prisoner."

Bilara raised her crystal ball high into the evening sky and murmured a few words. The sky grew dark, and large, black clouds rapidly gathered above Dragon Cliff. "We are happy to let Surah go!" shouted Turag mockingly, pushing the elf to the edge of the cliff. "Fly to your family," he ordered. "They are waiting for you." "Don't do it!" screamed Sera. "It's already much too dark. You'll fall to your death." Bilara raised her hands imploringly. There was a mighty roll of thunder and pieces of rock fell from the peak to where the Sun Elves were standing. They were just able to jump away in time, otherwise they would have been crushed. Bilara laughed again. "You cannot escape!" she called. "Today is the day of reckoning. If Surah dies, you too will perish." There was more thunder, and more rocks came crashing down. Surah was standing at the edge of the cliff, and felt her strength diminishing. The wind blew through her hair and she breathed deeply. Tears came to her eyes. She now knew who she was, but unfortunately this was the end for her. She looked around, heard the thunder from the distance and thought she could again see the little green bird through her eyes wet with tears. But it was only an illusion.

Surah knew she was about to die. However, her heart was free for she had solved the riddle of her ancestry. On the horizon, beyond the great thunderclouds, the sun went down and a last sunbeam lit up her face. She spread her arms and wings and jumped from Dragon Cliff...

But the ray of light did not only touch her face, it also lit up her little bag of belongings that she always carried. In the bag was also the Book of Elves. The bag had meanwhile become so worn that the ray of light shone directly onto the little mirror on the binding of the book. The light was reflected directly onto... the little green bird. Surah had thought she would never see it again, but it had only crept away into her bag when the elf was being taken through the cave passages by the shadowy figures. When the light struck the bird, it went up in flames, and from the flames arose a great, silver dragon.

As she fell, Surah had lost consciousness, so she did not see this transformation. The Sun Elves around Eyela screamed, but they could only watch powerlessly as Surah fell into the depths. Sera clutched her face in her hands.

Then they saw the silver dragon spread its giant wings. It also fell and it seemed to follow Surah with all the weight and strength of its entire body. At the last moment before Surah was about to smash into a jagged rock, the dragon stretched out its paw and seized the elf. It clutched her hair and pulled her up.

In horror, Turag, Bilara, Ophira and the other Shadow Elves had watched the drama unfold. Bilara, the sorceress, gave out a frightful curse. The mountain trembled and great rocks crashed down into the valley.

The great silver dragon turned round and now flew towards the group of Shadow Elves. It stopped in mid-air directly in front of them, flapping its giant wings. Bilara raised her crystal ball and wanted to make a curse, but she did not have the chance. The dragon opened its great mouth and spat fire at the group of Shadow Elves. When the flames and smoke had cleared, a strange spectacle was revealed. All the Shadow Elves stood in a row at the edge of the cliff and had been turned to stone. The silhouette of them wildly gesticulating and trying to defy the dragon made a bizarre, black contrast against the red evening sky.

Joy and Sorrow

The next morning, the sun rose radiantly behind the mountains and hills around Dragon Cliff. The whole night a gentle breeze had been blowing from the south and had driven the mist away to the north. It had not been so clear in this region for many years.

Eyela awoke and gazed around in astonishment, for the landscape was beautiful. High mountains and gentle green hills were interspersed with large meadows. In between, to the south, many small forests and narrow, clear streams could be seen.

The previous evening, the silver dragon had put the unconscious Surah down with the Sun Elves and had then flown off toward Oracle Mountain. Eyela and her friends had then spread their blankets between the horses to form a kind of tent to make a temporary resting place for the night.

By morning Surah had still not regained consciousness, but she was breathing evenly and her heartbeat was calm. Sera lay directly beside her and held her hand. She had made herbal bandages for her sister using special plants that she had brought from home.

Eyela observed them carefully. Outwardly they seemed very similar, apart from the different clothing. But whereas Sera had the charm of a pretty young elf girl, her twin sister clearly showed the signs of the fear and exertion of her recent adventure. Also her skin was very pale and her hair hung over her face in tangled strands.

Falaroy and Feya were meanwhile standing beside Eyela and could not help smiling when they saw the two sisters lying side by side so harmoniously.

At that moment Sera awoke, and Surah also gradually recovered her senses. Surah blinked into the sun. "Where am I?" she asked in amazement. Sera took her into her arms. "You're with your family," she said simply, with tears running down her cheeks. The friends then all sat down on a blanket, ate a little and told Surah all she wanted to know of her ancestry. "Jaro really was right," she said when the story was finished. "He prophesied that I was of royal descent." Surah briefly related her encounter with the elf boy and the others were astonished at everything that had befallen her. "Come, I will give you some beautiful new clothes," Eyela suggested. "Yours are completely ragged. Then we will pack our things and set off. I want to leave this place before dark." She cast a worried glance to the edge of the cliff where the stone figures of the Shadow Elves stood. But they looked as if no magic in the world could ever bring them back to life.

A little later, the elves were riding together down the same path on which they had come. Sera's horse was the strongest, so it had no trouble carrying the two sisters. Surah was now wearing a pretty robe, and in the sunshine she had already lost some of her pallor. But not only her skin, also her hair and especially her wings now shimmered colourfully in the midday sun.

They were all homesick for Summergreen House, and Surah was eager to find out what it was like there. But they had a long ride before them, for who knew whether chance, in the form of a Moon Elf or another magical creature, would again help them?

At a shallow pond in a dark forest, an elf knelt down to wash the dirt from her arms and legs. It was Nuray, the dark ruler. Tears ran down her face.

By a miracle she had been able to escape the flames of the River of Fire when the effect of Bilara's protective magic had worn off. At the last moment, when her robe was already burning, the dark ruler had managed to grab hold of one of the two elf-ice boats drifting on the lava flow. She had cleverly pulled it over her boat, thus creating a space where the fire could not penetrate. The time during which she was exposed to the waves and the flames of the River of Fire seemed an eternity to Nuray. She was tossed to and fro, and new side channels kept appearing into which Nuray drifted. But at length the river became narrower, and then completely ceased.

The dark ruler breathed heavily as she pushed aside the boat that had served as her roof. She set foot on land and noticed that the ground was still very hot. Her feet were burning and she ran quickly to escape from the solidified lava. Nuray was afraid, for she sensed that she was still deep below ground. In the cave passages that led away from this point there was total darkness. Hour after hour, Nuray felt her way forwards without knowing whether she would ever find her way back above ground. At times she had to crawl, as the passages were so narrow that there was barely space for a body to pass through. And then moisture penetrated from above, and Nuray had to wade knee-deep through water.

The dark ruler was close to despair. She shouted, but who was down there to hear? In the darkness, her hands grabbed something that might give her new hope. It was the thick, gnarled roots of large trees that had penetrated into the earth and jutted into the hollow passageways. Nuray realised that she could only be a little way beneath the surface. She felt her way further, and indeed soon noticed that the narrow passage she had entered led upwards. Weak light penetrated between the thick roots and claylike earth. Nuray seized the roots and pulled them apart. With her bare hands she dug her way through the gnarled wood until she could pull herself out into the open.

The pond beside which Nuray was now sitting gave her the chance to wash and cool her wounds. When she had again composed her thoughts, great bitterness took hold of her heart. Turag had betrayed her, but what was even worse was that Uhara had kept the secret of the story of her brother from her. Nuray's tears dropped into the grey pond. "Mother, how could you do it to me," she sobbed. She saw her own contorted face reflected in the water.

Suddenly the expression changed. The face became older and the skin much paler. "Is it you, mother?" asked Nuray in despair, for she thought she recognised the contours of Uhara's face. She heard a soft voice. "Don't cry, Nuray," she heard her say. "You have escaped your doom, even though you don't know it. Go to the north. Your horse is waiting for you at the edge of the forest. It will take you back to your palace in the Shadow Kingdom." Then the voice fell silent.

Table of Contents

page

The Land of the Elves..7

The Fateful Night..11

The Mysterious Dragon's Head............................17

The Great Festival..27

The Pact with the Dragons...................................36

The Mysterious Hall...45

Surah and Shadow Rock.......................................53

In the Kingdom of Mist...63

The Tree Gateway..72

The Pyramid in the Forest.....................................80

The Voice of the Oracle...90

Surah's Secret..99

page

Light and Shadow..109

The Face in the Mirror.......................................119

The Book of Elves...128

On Twisting Paths...139

Starry Sky..149

The Elf Spirits...159

In the Crater of the Volcano................................168

Turag..178

The Sun on the Horizon......................................188

The Wall of Mist..197

Sera and Surah..205

Joy and Sorrow..216

The author

Gecko Keck has been writing books and creating characters for children, youths and adults for almost two decades. As the creator of many fantasy games and stories, in recent years he has earned an international reputation and his work is known to a wide public. But he also loves the liberal arts.

He has shared his knowledge with interested readers and listeners in several published books and seminars.

At heart, Gecko Keck has always remained a child, which is why he sees his most important task as encouraging children's fantasy and creative thinking, not least in his own little daughter. That is why the artist particularly loves the world of the elves. "The symbolism behind the figures and stories fascinates me", says the author. "The lightness and transparency of an elf, in contrast to the magical strength of its character, inspire me daily in my work."